MAIL ORDER
Mix~Up

BRIDES OF SEATTLE – BOOK 3

CYNTHIA WOOLF

MAIL ORDER MIX-UP
Copyright © 2018 Cynthia Woolf

ISBN-13: 978-1-947075-54-2

MAIL ORDER MIX-UP is a work of fiction. Names, characters, places, brands, media and incidents either are the product of the author's imagination or are used fictitiously. Any resemblance to actual persons, living or dead, events, or locales, is entirely coincidental.

Published by Firehouse Publishing
Digital formatting: Author E.M.S.

Books written by Cynthia Woolf can be obtained either through the author's official website or through select, online book retailers.
www.cynthiawoolf.com

Books by Cynthia Woolf

BRIDES OF SEATTLE
Mail Order Mystery
Mail Order Mayhem
Mail Order Mix-Up

CENTRAL CITY BRIDES
The Dancing Bride
The Sapphire Bride
The Irish Bride
The Pretender Bride

KINDLE WORLDS
A Family for Christmas
Kissed by a Stranger
Thorpe's Mail-Order Bride

HOPE'S CROSSING
The Hunter Bride
The Replacement Bride
The Stolen Bride
The Unexpected Bride

AMERICAN MAIL-ORDER BRIDES
Genevieve, Bride of Nevada

THE SURPRISE BRIDES
Gideon

THE BRIDES OF TOMBSTONE
Mail Order Outlaw
Mail Order Doctor
Mail Order Baron

CHAPTER 1

August 2, 1865

Gabe Talbot walked around the horses outside his oldest brother Jason's barn and hitched the team to the wagon. Until recently this house and barn had been his, too. But now he was twenty-eight years old and decided he needed his own house. He had a small cabin about halfway between Jason's home, half way up Bridal Veil Mountain, and Seattle, on the shore of Puget Sound down below. Just minutes by buggy to either place.

He looked over at Jason who stood in front of the team, the sun bouncing off the golden streaks in his hair making his brown color seem blond. He was scratching behind the big black's ears. The tall appaloosa would be next. They were a good match in height and strength, if not in color. "Tell me

1

again why we're moving these two women to Seattle."

"Because our dear sister-in-law Lucy has sort of adopted them." He moved to the handsome white horse with the reddish brown spots over its flank. "She says they were abused by Harvey Long, too, even though they are his mother and younger sister."

"How does Lucy figure that? Good grief, Harvey Long nearly killed her, several times. He even shot her the last time."

"Because he left them to fend for themselves when we bought the mountain. He killed the mother's husband, the man who sold us the land, and stole the money from the sale, leaving them destitute."

The sun beat down and even at this early hour of the morning, the heat was already high, making sweat run in rivulets down his back. Even the scalp under his dark blond hair felt sweaty and it was just the start of the day. What he wouldn't give for a nice cool breeze. "Where will they live in Seattle?"

"One of those houses we built for the lumberjacks when they marry. Lucy says that's the least we can do."

"But we didn't do anything wrong, did we?"

"Not precisely, but if you think Drew is telling his newly pregnant wife, who is still recovering from that gunshot, by the way, that she can't move these women or help them, you're crazy."

2

"Lucy's expecting? That's great. When is the big event?"

"Not for about six and a half months. They've got plenty of time to prepare."

Gabe finished with the harness and the wagon was ready for Lucy and Drew. He turned back to Jason. "Let's get our horses." They walked back into the barn. "Aren't you and Rachel expecting about the same time?"

Both of their mounts were already saddled. Gabe followed Jason out into the barn yard where the wagon waited.

Jason put the reins over his saddle while they waited, standing by the wagon. "Yes. The babies should be very close together, which is great. They'll be able to play with each other when they're older. What about you? That cabin is a pretty small place to raise a family."

Gabe frowned and rolled his eyes. "What family? It's just me, and I don't expect that to change anytime soon. I've no desire to get married. I've walked out with a few of the brides but never with any intention to get hitched. Are you planning on filling all seven bedrooms in this house after all of us have gone?"

"If Rachel has her way, then yes. She comes from a big family, too, and wants lots of kids. She says it's not fair to Billy to be the only child and responsible for us in our old age. How many of the mail-order brides have you had outings with?"

"Just three. Even if I was looking for a wife, I haven't found the one who is right for me. Each one of them had something that made me say, "No, she's not the one.""

"Like what?"

"Well, Clara Simms talked too much. I don't think I got in two whole sentences the entire evening. Sadie James was too shy. She was just the opposite of Clara. Sadie didn't talk at all. Finally, Violet Richardson was too forward. Call me old-fashioned but I want to do the chasing, not the other way around."

Their brother Drew and his wife Lucy came out of the house and walked over to them.

Lucy, was just a little thing with dark almost black hair and today she was resplendent in a pretty pink dress. She stopped beside the wagon. "Are you gentlemen ready to go? It'll take a few hours with the wagon to get there."

Drew was his baby brother and out of the five of them he had the darkest brown hair. His light green eyes had every woman he met, swooning, until Lucy came along. Then he only had eyes for her. He stood behind Lucy and pulled her to him. "Ah, the dulcet tones of my lady wife."

Gabe watched as she turned around and leaned back in Drew's arms, completely trusting he would hold her and not let her fall. At times like this when he saw how happy his brothers were, Gabe felt a twinge of jealousy at their happiness, but not

4

enough to find him a wife and get married. He wasn't quite ready for that despite what he led his brothers to believe. He took one of the brides out occasionally so his brothers wouldn't badger him about finding a wife, but he never stepped out with the same woman twice.

Lucy's words brought him out of his reverie.

"You know, ever since you told me you found them, I've been anxious to meet them."

Drew smiled indulgently at Lucy. "I know. Gabe has the team already hitched to the wagon and their horses are saddled so we can go whenever you're ready."

"I am now." She released him and stepped back, out of his arms.

"All right. Let me help you into the wagon."

Lucy moved up to the side of the buckboard and Drew lifted her onto the seat. Then he climbed in beside her and picked up the reins.

"Are we all ready?"

"Yes. Let's go," said Jason, their oldest brother, as he rode to get in front of the wagon.

Gabe swung into the saddle of his horse, Buttons, not wanting to eat the dust the team pulling the wagon would kick up.

They followed the trail around Bridal Veil Mountain. The path wound through the heavy timber of the virgin forest. Someday, his brothers would harvest this timber, too, though they tried not to clear cut, but instead leaving the smallest trees to grow in the light now that they weren't in the shadow of the large timber.

The trail ended near a little ramshackle cabin that Gabe was sure was even smaller than his. He'd bet it was only three rooms. Probably, two bedrooms in the back and the kitchen, dining, and living rooms all together in one big room in the front half. The building was just too small for anything else.

Drew pulled the wagon around so that the back of the bed was nearest the cabin's door. Then he got down, and after helping Lucy off the buckboard, they crossed the yard to the cabin. Gabe and Jason waited on their horses since Drew was the one who'd met the women before.

A white-haired woman came out to greet them.

"Mr. Talbot," she said, holding out her hand to Drew. "I wasn't sure you'd come."

He cocked his head to one side. "Why is that, Mrs. Parker?"

She gave a slight shake of her head. "Just wouldn't be the first time someone promised us something that didn't come to pass. And please call me, Wilma."

"You'll find, Wilma, that we Talbots, keep our word."

She chuckled. "So you do. And who do you have with you?"

Drew put his arm around Lucy's shoulders.

"Forgive me. This is my wife, Lucy."

Lucy stepped forward and held out her hand. "I'm very pleased to meet you, Wilma."

"You, too. I'm sorry for what you endured at Harvey's hands, Mrs. Talbot—"

"Lucy, please."

"Well, Lucy, he was always an evil child. I hadn't been able to manage him since he was a boy."

"From what Drew told me, you suffered mightily at Harvey's hands as did I."

That's when Gabe saw her and all the conversation between Drew, Lucy, and the Parker woman faded to the background. The vision was a tall, slender woman, with dark brown hair and brown eyes. She came out of the cabin wearing a plaid man's shirt and wool pants. Her hair was pulled back into a single braid that fell over her shoulder almost to her waist. She was pretty but not in the classical sense. Her face had strong lines, a firm jaw and high cheek bones, but she attracted Gabe like no one ever had before, despite her men's clothes. Clothes which fit very well. Suddenly he was very happy his little brother had roped him into this excursion.

She went directly up to Lucy and held out her hand. "Josie Long."

Josie. A beautiful name.

Lucy shook her hand with both of hers. "Miss Long, very pleased to meet you."

Josie lifted an eyebrow and cocked her head to the side while looking down at Lucy who was several inches shorter. "Why are you being so nice to us, Mrs. Talbot? Most folks wouldn't want to help us after what Harvey did to you."

Gabe had wondered this himself since Harvey had beat Lucy up and shot her nearly killing her. But Drew explained to him the night before that Lucy was that way. She hated to see anyone suffer and if there was a way she could help she would.

"When Harvey bragged to me about what he'd done to you and then Drew told me about you," said Lucy. "I knew we had to help. Harvey abused you two as much as he did me, maybe more."

"He did at that," said Wilma Parker. "We know he fled with the money from the sale of Bridal Veil Mountain, but we aren't sure about Elias, do you know? It would set my mind at ease."

"Yes, ma'am. I'm so sorry but Harvey told me he killed Elias and buried him here on the mountain but I don't know where."

"Didn't I tell you, Mama?" Josie looked over to Lucy and Drew. "I knew he did away with him." She put an arm around her mother's shoulders. "He was jealous because Mama was happy again."

Gabe couldn't wait any longer and walked up to Drew's side.

"Drew, won't you introduce us?" Gabe kept his eyes on Josie and saw the widening of her eyes when she looked at him. *That's good, very good. She's interested. She's not shy like Sadie James. She says what's on her mind but is not overly talkative like Clara*

Simms and if she wants to chase me like Violet Richardson, I just might let her catch me.

Drew stepped back and Gabe filled the empty space, his gaze never leaving hers.

"Oh, of course. Mrs. Parker, Miss Long." Drew clapped Gabe on the back. "This is my older brother, Gabe, and the man on the horse is my oldest brother, Jason. I'm the baby of the family."

"Pleased to meet you both," Jason called out.

Gabe stepped forward and shook hands with Mrs. Parker. "Happy to meet you, ma'am."

Then he turned to Josie and put out his hand. "Miss Long. Very delighted to make your acquaintance."

The bolt of lightning that shot through him when she took his hand shocked him to his core. Her eyes widened even further, her nostrils flared. She tried to pull away, but Gabe held her, gently. "Very pleased, indeed."

"You can release me now, Mr. Talbot."

Her voice was a sultry and low whisper, as though she wanted only him to hear. Reluctantly, he opened his hand, and she slowly slid her hand away, feeling him with her fingers as she moved.

Jason came near and slapped him on the back. "Shall we get these ladies loaded and in their new home?"

"Yes, we shall." *I'm glad you'll be closer, Josie Long. I'd like to get to know you better.*

With all of them pitching in except Lucy, who was still recovering from a gunshot wound received from Harvey Long, they were finished loading the wagon in about an hour.

Gabe and Josie went through the three rooms, checking each one for something they missed.

"Is that all of it?" asked Gabe.

Josie walked to the sink and reached under it. She came out with a bunch of carrots. "Yes. That's everything."

They walked out to the front of the house where Wilma stood holding the reins for two horses. The animals looked well cared for and, unlike the cabin, looked like prime stock."

"You have beautiful mounts," said Gabe.

Josie raised her chin a little and smiled. "One thing my father taught us—don't skimp when buying horses. They'll save your life one day."

Gabe nodded. "He was right. I can appreciate when someone knows good horseflesh and how to care for them. Shall we go?"

"Yes."

He watched her walk to her animal. She greeted the horse like an old friend, patted his nose and gave him a carrot as a treat and put the rest of the vegetables in her saddlebags. Then she mounted and looked at ease like she was part of the animal.

He mounted and brought his horse next to hers.

"What's your horse's name?"

"He's called Storm because his color is a cloudy gray."

"My horse is Buttons. My nephew named him. Billy was just three."

She chuckled. "It was nice of you not to change it."

"Oh, I couldn't. He would have been heartbroken. Shall we lead the way to Seattle?" *That seems so long ago and it was just seven years. He's changed so much from a little tow-haired boy to an eleven-year-old who is almost too smart for his own britches. He's so bright. He won't be a logger, he'll be a scientist or a teacher maybe.*

"Yes, let's go."

The trek was slow with the horses pulling the full wagon only able to walk, so it took about three hours to get to Seattle from the west side of the mountain.

Gabe and Josie led the way to Seattle followed by Jason, Wilma and the wagon.

"So Gabe, what do you do for a living?"

"Four of my brothers and I run the lumber company just outside of Seattle."

"How many brothers do you have?"

"There are five of us brothers and we have one sister back east."

"I heard you brought in a bunch of women to be brides for your workers."

"We did. One hundred of them came with us from Massachusetts. All of them willing to make the trip for the chance of marriage and family."

"What about you? Are you looking for a wife out of the hundred?"

He watched her carefully and was surprised by the question?

"No, that would be a mistake, a terrible mix-up if one of the brides thought she was going to marry me. I haven't had the desire to marry." *Until now.*

She cocked her head to the side, but didn't say anything.

"None of us expected to find our wives among the women, yet both Jason and Drew have done just that. You just met Lucy and Jason's wife, Rachel, was also one of the brides. What do you like to do for fun?"

"I hadn't thought about it. Mama and I don't have much time for fun. Mostly we just did what we needed to survive. I've been taking care of us for the last ten years, since I was thirteen. But I guess more than anything I like to ride. When I go to Seattle, Storm and I ride around on the beach. The sand lets us have more freedom to run than any other time. What about you?"

"I like to hunt and fish, for pleasure as well as for food."

"Well, I guess I do, too, now that you mention it. When I have free time, I usually pack a lunch and go to one of my favorite fishing spots and spend the day. I don't do things like knit or crochet. I never learned how and never wanted to learn."

Gabe and Josie talked almost the entire way back to Seattle. He was a bit surprised when he saw the little enclave of five houses in front of them. The time had gone quickly. He and the other riders pulled their horses to the side and let the wagon pass by.

At the moment all the homes were vacant, and each had the same floor plan with four rooms—two bedrooms, a kitchen and a living room. Each was furnished with a stove, icebox, table, and chairs in the kitchen, though no water pump sat on the sink. They would have to haul water from the community well.

In the living room, a sofa and an overstuffed chair stood in front of the fireplace. Frilly calico curtains were on all the windows, courtesy of the brides.

He, Jason, Josie and Wilma tied their horses to the hitching rail out in front of the house. Then they waited for Drew and Lucy before going inside.

"The house isn't large, but I believe it's bigger than what you had. I hope you like it," said Jason to Wilma and Josie.

"I'm sure we'll love it, Mr. Talbot," said Wilma.

Gabe looked over at Josie. She was smiling, and her eyes sparkled. He'd like to see her looking at him like that.

Just that quick he went from never wanting to get married to wanting Josie for his bride. Now to convince her.

After unloading the wagon full of the furniture which included two of everything from the bedrooms—bed, chest of drawers, nightstand and commode. From the living room they'd brought two hand carved rocking chairs and a couple of tables just big enough to hold a lamp and a book.

"Would any of you like a cup of tea?" asked Wilma. "I've got the kitchen situated, and we have a kettle, water, and tea, with enough cups for everyone."

"I'd like some," said Gabe, as he watched Josie help her mother. He'd stay for a cup of water straight from a mud puddle if it meant being around Josie.

"That would be very nice," said Lucy. "I could use a cup of tea. I'm afraid, even though I didn't do anything, but watch, I'm still tired. As my husband said," she looked up at Drew. "I haven't recovered enough for this to be my first outing, but I wouldn't have missed it for anything."

Shortly, the tea kettle whistled, and Wilma prepared the tea for everyone.

Jason sat at the table next to Wilma. "What do you plan on doing now that you're living here? The same as before? Hunting and fishing to make a living?"

"I hadn't given it much thought, to be honest," said Wilma. "Josie used to sell fresh and smoked meat and fish to a butcher in Tacoma. But here we don't have a smokehouse."

Gabe and Josie leaned against the counter with their backs to the cupboards.

"I'm sure the butcher would buy the fresh meat," said Jason. "I just thought that given the opportunity, you might want to do something else."

After his conversation with Josie, Gabe wondered what else she'd be able to do. She wouldn't be taking in laundry, that's for sure.

Wilma stopped pouring and thought a moment before speaking to Jason. "Well, your wife and Drew's Lucy will be turning Josie here into a female so she can catch a husband. Ain't that right?"

Josie rolled her eyes at her mother. "I'm a girl, Mama. I just don't dress like one and I don't intend to start now."

"I don't see anything wrong with the way Josie looks," said Gabe. He smiled and winked at Josie.

What am I thinking? I've only taken the brides for walks to keep the brothers off my back. Josie is not the kind of woman to be trifled with, not without thought to marriage. But after what happened with Marian, I must not be good husband material. Marian hated the arrangement her father made so much that after I tried to kiss her she became a nun to avoid marriage. If I'm so unloveable, how can I even consider courting Josie? And yet, I've never been so drawn to a woman before.

What if she rejects me like Marian did? Will she walk away rather than accept a hug or kiss from me?

I've seen what marriage can do when it's with someone you love. Jason was devastated when Cassie died because he loved her. Yet, next to my parents, they had one of the best marriages I've ever seen. Now, I see him with Rachel and Drew with Lucy and they obviously love each other and are very happy. But how do they put their fears behind them and fall in love again?

Perhaps Josie and I could be friends. I'm not ready to ignore the feelings I have. They are too strong, too important to ignore.

Josie turned beet red and dropped her gaze to the floor.

Lucy looked up at Gabe, lifted an eyebrow, cocked her head to the side and narrowed her gaze.

"That's interesting," she said before returning her attention to those at the table.

Jason put his cup in the sink. "I'm afraid we need to leave. My wife is expecting me home in time for supper, the three of you as well." He jutted his chin toward Gabe, Drew and Lucy in turn.

"He's right. I need to help Rachel," said Lucy.

"You need to go to bed and rest," corrected Drew.

Lucy's mouth turned down and her eyebrows furrowed in a pout.

Gabe wasn't ready to leave Josie's company. "Ladies. You two don't have anything to prepare for supper. Why not let me take you to eat at the Seattle Inn?"

"No," said Josie, immediately.

I will not take this personally. She doesn't know me well enough to dislike me yet, though she may do just that later.

"Well," Wilma looked between Josie and Gabe, and then grinned. "I do believe that would be really nice. Now Josie, wash up and then we'll go."

"Mama—"

Wilma's gaze narrowed and lines formed between her brows. "Don't give me no guff, girl. Wash your face so we can go eat."

Josie looked at Gabe with daggers in her eyes. He just smiled back. He'd get down to why she found spending time with him so objectionable, but for now he was happy she was joining him for supper.

Drew shook his head, Lucy grinned and so did Jason. Then they left Gabe with the two women.

When Josie had washed her face and hands, the three of them walked two blocks down the hill to the Inn.

The restaurant in the Inn was excellent and almost always busy, full of lumberjacks and now brides, who got tired of eating their own cooking.

If he and his brothers had not imported one hundred women from the east as brides for their employees, the restaurant would be full of men. The only women in town before were Dolly and the two girls, Mazie and Trixie, she employed to entertain the men but not as prostitutes, just as saloon girls. Though what the girls did on their own time, Gabe could only guess.

The Talbots provided meals for the lumberjacks at camp, but the offerings often depended on the mood of the cook. Sometimes they were delicious, and occasionally, they were bad.

Tonight, the establishment was packed. Almost every one of the red-checked tablecloth covered tables was full. The only one available was right in front of the window. Gabe didn't like the idea of putting Josie and Wilma on exhibit.

"Could you close the curtains, please, miss?" he asked the waitress, who handed them each a menu.

"What's the matter, Mr. Talbot. Don't want to be seen with us?"

Josie's tone challenged him to deny it. He lifted an eyebrow but wondered what he'd done to make her so combative. "I simply didn't want you to feel like I was putting you on display. But if you don't mind, I certainly don't. I'm quite happy letting everyone know I'm having supper with two beautiful women."

Josie opened her mouth to say something and then closed it.

The waitress waited to close the curtain and finally did when Josie was left speechless. "I'll be back in a few minutes to take your order."

Wilma laughed. "It's not too often that my Josie is at a loss for words. Congratulations, Mr. Talbot."

Gabe chuckled. "Can we please drop the Mr. Talbot? I'd like to be Gabe, just Gabe."

"That'd be fine. We're Wilma and Josie, which is so much easier."

"I agree. Now, do you know what you'd like to eat?"

"I'd like fried chicken," said Wilma. "We ate the last of our chickens this time a year ago and they never got replaced. Just as well, I guess. We couldn't keep them in town."

"I don't know why not. We'll have to have a barn built for your horses, so why not a chicken coop, too? I'll get the men on it right away. They can just add the coop to one side of the barn so basically it'll be all one building not two."

"We don't have any way to pay for a chicken coop much less a barn, *Mr. Talbot*."

"Well, uh, it comes with the house."

The waitress returned and took their orders.

Gabe had said the first thing that came to his mind. He couldn't seem to take his gaze off Josie, but realizing he was being rude, staring like he was, and forced himself to stop. But he'd never seen anyone who looked like her. She was interesting. Her eyes reminded him of his favorite brandy when it was heated just enough and vapors filled the glass, making the brown liquid shimmer. Her nose was small and turned up the slightest bit at the end. Her cheekbones were high and somewhat angular. But her lips were her greatest

19

asset, when they weren't turned down in a frown. They were perfect, heart-shaped and pink as an early rose bud.

He looked at Wilma, who smiled and nodded. She was obviously pleased with the attention he showed her daughter.

But Josie? One look at the mutiny in her eyes told him she would rather be anywhere but here... with him.

He should be glad she didn't want anything to do with him but he couldn't forget the feeling, the lightning that ran through him at her first touch. He'd never experienced anything that intense before and he was sure she felt it, too. Feelings that strong definitely needed exploring, didn't they? But this strong attraction certainly didn't mean he was looking at falling in love. No, not at all. Not him. Not after Marian. Never would he go through that kind of pain again.

CHAPTER 2

After supper, Josie allowed Gabe to walk them back to their new house.

"Why don't you two young people sit out here on the swing for a spell," said her mother. "I've got things to do inside."

Josie stared at her mother's back as she walked into the house. The woman was practically throwing her at Gabe. No way did she want anything to do with the infernal man. Her mother didn't even let her clean anything but her hands and face. Her hair was a mess, the braid coming undone, so she re-braided it to one side as they walked.

What were he and Mama thinking? Had they planned this? No. Her mother hadn't even known of Gabe Talbot before today.

Josie stayed standing and crossed her arms over her chest. "What do you want, Mr. Talbot?

He sat back in the swing and eyed her. "Are we putting our cards on the table? Very well. I want to get to know you, perhaps even court you. What do you think about that?"

His gaze traveled over her, scorching her beneath his stare. At his statement, if she hadn't been leaning on the porch railing, she'd be on the floor.

She snorted. "Don't be ridiculous? You don't even know me."

Gabe just sat with a big grin on his face, the smile never wavering.

I can't decide if he's happy or his brain is addled.

"So let's get to know each other. Then you can make up your mind."

She thought about his suggestion for a moment. *I know he's looking for a romantic relationship but I don't want any man to tell me what to do. Oh, he can try, but he's in for a shock.* "Take me fishing a week from today, and we'll talk more about it."

"Why wait a week?"

She shrugged. "Because I've got obligations. I'm headed to Olympia tomorrow morning for supplies and won't be back for about five days. So do we have a date?"

"You can get supplies here in Seattle, why go to Olympia?"

She crossed her arms over her chest. "Because I've already paid for the supplies in Olympia. Not that it is any of your business."

"You're right. Your business is your business and you've got a deal. Fishing next week." He stood and held out his hand.

She stared at his outstretched hand, narrowed her gaze and cocked her head before deciding no harm would be done by taking his hand.

He brought her hand to his lips, turned it over and kissed the underside of her wrist. That was all. Just a gentle, sweet kiss on her wrist that sent shivers up and down her spine.

When he let go of her hand, she looked at it, almost expecting a mark to show where he'd seared her, though she had no pain, only pleasure.

Gabe chuckled.

At the sound, her head jerked up, and she stared at him.

"I didn't give you permission to kiss me…anywhere? Why did you do that? You gave me shivers."

"I would apologize, but you have delectable wrists and I just couldn't resist. I'm glad to know that my kisses can affect you. It would appear that you are a passionate woman, Josie Long. Yes, indeed."

Josie stood still as she watched him walk away. What kind of man was he?

A week later Josie waited beside Storm who was saddled and ready to go. She had put all of her equipment on Storm and laid the reins over the hitching rail. The horse was well trained not to move. She found herself anxious for this excursion. The entire trip to Olympia, Gabe invaded her thoughts and at times her dreams. She couldn't decide if she liked him or was just infuriated by him.

Gabe rode up on a magnificent piece of horse flesh. The beautiful black stallion looked almost as good as Storm.

"That's a different horse than you rode last week. He's very handsome, not that Buttons wasn't, but this horse turns heads when he passes."

"Thanks. This is Star, so named for—"

She grinned and pointed to the horse's head. "The white star on his forehead."

Gabe smiled. "Yes, that's right. Billy was older when he named this horse."

"Why aren't you riding Buttons?"

"Billy's riding him today. He and a friend are also going fishing today, too, and Buttons is the gentlest horse we have. You look like you're ready to go." He crossed his arms on the saddle horn and leaned forward. "Better take a coat. We might get rained on."

She cocked her head to the side. "This is Seattle. Of course, we'll get rained on. I've got my slicker in the saddlebags."

"Good. I brought lunch. When I dropped off Buttons for Billy, Rachel and Lucy wouldn't let me out of the house until they'd packed enough food for six people. Trust me; we could be lost for a week and not go hungry."

Josie laughed. He'd done it again. How did he always make her laugh? Not that she was complaining, she liked it. Laughing made her feel young and carefree, something she hadn't been since her stepfather, Elias Parker, disappeared ten years ago and she'd had to take over for him or starve.

"Come on. The place I want to go is a bit far from here. It'll take us a little more than an hour, and that's galloping as much as possible without hurting our horses. Are you ready?"

"Yes, ma'am."

"Let's go." She clicked her tongue and Storm began walking. Once they reached the top of the hill, she took the right fork in the road. This road was almost flat. She clicked her tongue again. This time the horse picked up the pace going from a walk to a trot and finally to a smooth lope.

Josie kept them to that pace for about ten minutes; then she reined back Storm until he was just walking.

The horses walked side by side. When they galloped, Josie was in front.

Josie rested her hand holding the reins on top of the saddle horn. "So Gabe, have you been here since the Talbots bought Bridal Veil Mountain from Elias?"

"Yes, all of us, my four brothers and me, came out here from New Bedford, Massachusetts together. Our parents were dead and our baby sister had just gotten married. But the main reason was that Jason's wife, Cassie, had recently died in childbirth. Jason had to get away and we went with him. We were all sort of adventurers at the time. And nothing was holding us there. Besides, Jason was determined to come and he had a new baby. We couldn't let him go by himself."

"That's awfully nice of you. Did you have a girl back there?"

"I was engaged to be married but plans changed."

"Something you want to talk about?"

"No. Not at this time."

Josie shrugged. "That's fine for now. If we get closer, I'll need to know. For now we need to gallop again. Follow me."

She touched her heels to Storm's sides and clicked her tongue twice. The horse answered the commands and took off galloping in short order. She kept that speed for about ten minutes. She did that whole routine twice more.

Josie slowed. The path was coming up and she knew if she wasn't careful she'd miss it. The trail was so overgrown with weeds and grasses if she hadn't known it was there, she'd have ridden right by.

She kept the horses to a walk. The path was too narrow and dangerous to travel any faster. Around a mile in, the trees parted, and a large beaver pond lay in front of them. She led them across a small creek and then about half way up the far side of the lake.

"Gabe do you see how clear the water is? How deep do you think the pool is?"

"Well, I can see the bottom so I figure it's a couple of feet deep."

"I remember the first time I was here and saw the bottom like this. I thought it was a shallow pond. Later in the day I learned quite differently. I'd gotten my fly stuck and waded out to retrieve it only to find that the water was at least six feet deep. I got an unexpected bath that day, but," she waggled her eyebrows and grinned. "I also got my favorite fly back." She waved her arm toward the water. "Well, what do you think? Can you manage to catch a few rainbows?"

He laughed. "Oh, yeah. I bet I catch more than you do."

She lifted an eyebrow. "You want to bet?"

"What are the stakes?"

She put her creel over her shoulder and took her fly rod out of the long, slender sack she kept the three pieces in. The pieces interlocked together to form a six foot rod. "If you win, you can court me with the result being marriage and I want a cook and a housekeeper. If I win, we don't get married and remain friends...only."

"Deal. Looks like we'll be getting married."

She grinned. "Looks to me like we'll be friends… only."

"We'll see."

They both dismounted and hobbled their horses.

Josie took her fly rod from its case and, with her flies in her pocket, headed to her favorite spot. Once there, she pulled some wet grass and put it in the bottom of her creel. It would keep the fish from drying out and sticking to the wicker bottom.

Gabe watched her and then walked to the opposite side of the lake. Because the pond wasn't huge, they'd both be fishing in about the same spot of water. She'd never shared this place with anyone before. *I wonder why I decided to bring him to my favorite fishing hole? Do I like him more than I'm willing to admit, even to myself?*

After casting a couple of times and bringing the fly in slowly each time, Josie was worried she might not win the contest. This was important to her and she wondered if she really wanted to win.

On the third cast, a fish struck the fly. She jerked up the front end of the rod, setting the hook, and then reeled in the fish.

Struggling, with the hook firmly in its jaw, the fish fought as she reeled it in. Her cane fly rod bending at the end under the weight of the fish, which was a nice twelve or thirteen-inch cutthroat trout. The easily recognizable fish was named that because of the orange slashes of color on the lower jaw.

Josie put her finger through the animal's gill, lifted it high, almost in triumph, and showed it to Gabe.

"Nice catch," called Gabe, just as a fish hit his fly.

She watched him set the hook, bring the fish in and put it in his creel.

"What did you get?"

"A bow," he yelled back.

"How big?"

"About a foot. Good sized fish."

Josie smiled and muttered under her breath. *Dang if we keep this up, no one will win, and I want to win this bet.*

They'd been fishing a couple of hours and seeing that the sun was directly over head, she knew it was around noon. That explained the growl of her stomach. Josie called over to Gabe. "How many fish do you have? I'm hungry and ready to stop for lunch. What did you bring to eat?"

"I'll be right over."

When he arrived, he stopped in front of her and showed her the three nice fish he caught.

"You have one more fish than I do. So at this point you've won, but I'll beat you after lunch. What did you bring? You said Rachel and Lucy had both packed food."

"I intend to stay ahead of you. I do want to court you, Josie. For real. Not as part of a bet, but if I have to take it as a win of a bet, I will. I'll take you however I can get you. As to lunch, I have no idea what they made. I just put it in my saddlebags."

"Hmpft. We're not done here."

As they approached the horses, Josie saw movement in the trees near the animals.

She reached over and grabbed his arm stopping their progress and pointed with her other hand. "Look! Did you see that?"

"What?"

"Something or someone in the trees near the horses."

"I didn't see anything."

They walked up to their animals.

"Hey, my saddle bags are missing." Gabe picked up the ties that had held his saddle bags.

"I knew I saw something. Come on. We're finding whoever stole that food."

She ran toward the place she'd seen the movement and looked around the ground.

Seeing tracks, she squatted down beside them. "These footprints are tiny, like a child's size. I don't have a good feeling about this. I usually never see anyone else up here. Let's follow them."

"Agreed."

They tracked the footprints through the thick forest, losing the trail and then finding them again and following until they saw a small, rough-hewn cabin that had definitely seen better days.

As they approached the shack, a rifle barrel appeared out of the window.

"What do you want?" shouted a young voice.

Josie and Gabe looked at each other. She didn't like having a gun pointed at her especially by someone who she thought sure was a child.

"We came to find whoever stole our lunch," called Josie.

"Wasn't nobody here."

"Well, we followed the tracks here," yelled Gabe. Under his breath, he said, "We need to get in there. That's just a kid with a scattergun. Something is wrong in that cabin."

"I agree," whispered Josie. "I'll keep their attention, and you go around back."

Josie started moving toward the cabin.

"Look whoever you are, no need to use the shotgun. We'll share. I'm coming up to the cabin."

"Stay where you are. I'll shoot."

Josie raised her hands and moved forward slowly but ever watchful of the gun pointed her way. She felt the sweat, from the warm day and her tense nerves, roll in rivulets between her breasts. Her hands shook and keeping her voice steady took concentration she wasn't feeling right now.

She kept looking over to where Gabe worked his way through the forest to the side of the house. Josie saw he was on the side of the house waiting for her.

"You don't want to shoot me. I just want to help you," she said as she walked forward. "Why don't you let me in and we can talk? You obviously need the food, or you wouldn't have stolen my lunch."

"No, we're fine. Hey, where'd that man go?"

Gabe came around from the side to the front of the house and stood beside the window out of the sight of the person in the cabin, Gabe grabbed the rifle barrel and pointed it upward. It went off, the buckshot going into the air.

The sound of the gunshot caused a baby inside to cry.

Josie rushed forward and opened the door. The window provided very little light, so she left the door open. When her eyes adjusted to the dimness of the interior, she saw that the cabin was one big room. Two boys, one as tall as the girl, Josie figured him to be about ten and a younger one, probably about six. The younger one hugged a baby tightly. The three of them huddled together next to the table in the middle of the room on which lay Gabe's saddlebags. A girl of about twelve or thirteen stood at the window, her hands still clutching the gun even though Gabe held fast to the barrel outside.

Josie went over, placed one hand on the girl's shoulder and the other on the gun, slowly lowering it.

"It's all right. You can let go now."

The girl relinquished the weapon and dissolved into tears. Her siblings cried out and ran to her.

Josie leaned the shotgun against the wall.

Gabe entered and shook his head. He crouched and talked to the huddled children. "What's your name? I'm Gabe Talbot and this is Josie Long."

The older boy stepped forward.

"I'm Walt Devlin." He pointed at each of his siblings in turn. "These are my sisters, Matilda and Etta, and my brother Bobby."

"My name is Mattie," the girl corrected her brother.

Walt shrugged. "Fine. Mattie."

Bobby held the little girl, Etta, who struggled to be let down. He put her on the dirt floor, and she toddled over to Josie where she raised her arms.

"Up."

Josie looked at Gabe for direction.

"She wants you to pick her up." Gabe pointed at the baby.

She took a step back. "Me? I don't know anything about kids."

"Just bend down and pick her up."

Josie looked down at the tiny girl who was dirty from head to toe. She put her hands under the child's arms and lifted her, holding Etta straight out in front of her.

Gabe chuckled. "Bend your elbows and bring the baby close. Cuddle with her."

She did, and as soon as Etta was close enough, she wrapped one arm around Josie's neck and rested her cheek on Josie's chest.

"Where are your parents?" asked Gabe as he stood.

"Mama's dead. Died birthin' Etta," said Mattie. The girl was a several inches shorter than Josie. She figured her to be under five feet. Just a little thing. Her dress was tattered and dirty. Her hair was brown. At least, Josie thought the color was brown. It was dirty and greasy. None of the kids looked like they'd had a bath in a year. The shack had a dirt floor, with sleeping pallets on one side of the room and the 'kitchen' on the other with a table in the middle, which held Gabe's saddle bags. A fireplace was both the source of heat and the method of cooking.

"Where is your father?" Gabe looked around and there was little sign of an adult. Even the sleeping pads were only for the kids. If an adult lived here at one time, he didn't now.

"He went hunting about five months ago and never came back. I figure he got killed by a bear or mountain lion," said Mattie.

"Do you have any other relatives or friends here in Seattle?"

Mattie shook her head. "We have an aunt and uncle back east somewhere but I haven't seen or heard from them in years."

"I see. How old are you all?" asked Gabe.

"I'm fourteen, Walt is eleven, Bobby is six and Etta is about thirteen months, she just started walking. It's hard to keep track of the days without a calendar."

The baby stunk. Josie crinkled her nose and did her best not to put the baby away from her, but the baby needed changing and a bath something terrible.

"When is the last time you all had a full meal or a bath and clean clothes?" asked Josie.

Tears filled the girl's eyes and rolled down her cheeks. "I done the best I could. But it's hard havin' to provide everything. Water is too far away to carry more' in a bucket at a time, and we need that to drink and eat. Washin' wasn't a need that could be taken care of except to go to the pond and bathe when the weather warmed up."

Gabe gazed at Mattie and Walt.

"How would you like to come back to Seattle with us? You'll get clean clothes, good food and beds to sleep in."

Josie's heart went out to these kids. They were abandoned and yet they stayed together. Mattie and Walt doing their best, just as Josie had done so many years ago. But Josie had a mother to help her. These kids had no one but each other.

Mattie and Walt glanced at each other and nodded.

"We'd like that," said Mattie.

Josie watched the kids and noticed all of their feet were bare.

"Do you have shoes?"

Mattie shook her head. "We was supposed to get some when Daddy got back."

"That's okay. We'll bring the horses here. We're riding to Seattle. Gabe you ready."

"If it's okay, we'd just as soon go with you now," said Walt.

Josie smiled and nodded. "Okay, that's fine. I guess you've been getting along with no shoes so far. No reason to try and save your feet from injury now. Do you want to take anything from this place? Because you won't be coming back here?"

Mattie shook her head and pulled out her skirt at the sides. "We're wearin' the only clothes we have. We ain't got nothin' to take."

"Let's go then." Josie led the way, carrying Etta, knowing that after this trip she would need a bath as much as the baby did.

Gabe grabbed his saddle bags from the table.

They reached the horses. Josie handed Etta to Mattie and retrieved their fishing equipment, the shen rode holding Etta with Mattie mounted behind her. Gabe held Bobby, and Walt sat behind the saddle.

They rode to Gabe's house. After they put the horses in the barn, they walked back to the house. As they walked, Gabe spoke softly.

"Josie, I think we need to bathe the kids first."

She shook her head. *I don't know much, but I do know those kids are hungry, desperately hungry to steal saddlebags from strangers.* "We need to feed them first. That lunch you had probably won't make a dent in their hunger. They didn't even have time to eat it. It looked to me like most of it was still in the saddlebags. What do you have to eat here?"

"Nothing. I don't cook. I go back to the family home for meals or eat at the lumber camp."

"Well, I suggest that you go to the restaurant. I'll get water boiling, bring your tub in and let the children bathe. You do have a bathtub, don't you?"

"Yes, I have a bathtub. It's in the barn. It's pretty heavy. I'll bring it in before I leave. You'll need buckets. There are two on the porch and two more in the barn."

"All right. While you're waiting for the food to be prepared, you can go to the mercantile and buy some clothes and whatever it is the baby wears on her bottom."

"They are changing cloths," said Mattie. "Haven't you ever changed a baby?"

"Good gracious, no. I've never been around kids of any kind. I'm just doing the logical thing of getting you all bathed."

"I changed Billy plenty when he was a baby," said Gabe. "I have a good idea what to get. I'll be back with the tub and the buckets from the barn, then I'll head to the mercantile and restaurant, as soon as possible."

After Gabe left, Josie turned to Mattie. "We're lucky. Gabe has water in the house. I'll get the buckets off the porch, too."

Josie went outside. She looked around and saw two metal buckets upside down on the porch. She brought them in, filled them and put them on the stove to heat. Seeing cobwebs in the tub she wiped them out with a hand towel she found in one of the kitchen drawers.

The kids sat at the table.

Josie could almost hear their stomachs growl.

"I'm sorry he didn't have any food. Let's see what was in those saddlebags. We'll make sure there is always food here from now on."

Josie opened the saddle bags and took out half a dozen sandwiches, a dozen cookies, a whole fried chicken, and a quart of apple cider.

"Well, it looks like there is enough to stop your stomachs from growling. Let me find plates and cups."

In short order she had the plates set out and the kids had dished up the food.

Josie saw that Mattie was feeding Etta but wasn't eating anything herself. "Do you want me to hold her so you can eat?"

Mattie shook her head. "I need to feed her as much as she'll eat first. I'll eat what's left."

Gabe came back with the tub and the buckets.

"Thank you," said Josie. "I'll get those filled and heating in a few minutes."

Gabe nodded. "I'll be back shortly."

Mattie gazed at Josie. "Where you goin' to put us to sleep?"

Josie put her finger on her chin and thought a moment. "Well, I thought the boys could stay here and the girls—"

"No." Mattie stood with her free hand fisted and holding Etta with her other arm. "You won't separate us. I won't allow it. I'd rather go back to the cabin and live like we was than have us separated."

"It wouldn't be permanent, Mattie. Just until—"

"No. We won't be separated. Period."

"All right. Don't fret. We'll figure out something."

I don't see how they will be able to stay together. They'll have to be separated for a short time until parents for them can be found. But where will we find parents willing to take in four children, four more mouths to feed, in this little town?

CHAPTER 3

Josie took the food from Gabe and added it to that on the table. He'd returned from the restaurant with two whole fried chickens, four quarts of stew, two loaves of bread, a crock of butter, and two apple pies.

By the time lunch was over, all the food was gone, including both pies. Josie had never seen anyone, including Gabe, that was as hungry as these kids.

"How did you survive out there for five months without your father?"

Mattie folded her arms across her chest.

"We just did."

"Well, I hope that everyone got full." Gabe patted his stomach. "I'll have to make another trip to the Inn for more food for supper tonight."

Josie thought Etta must think Gabe is her father the way the little girl clung to him. She took her and gave her to Mattie. "Would you give Etta a bath and put her in the new clothes that Gabe bought? After that you can bathe and then the boys. Washing up before we ate simply isn't enough. You all need real baths."

"Yes, I'll bathe Etta. Are you and Gabe married?"

"No." She was surprised that Gabe would step up like he has to help these kids. *Maybe I was wrong about him. Perhaps he isn't a self-centered son-of-a-gun.* She'd have to remember not to cuss anymore. Not around the kids. *I wonder if Mama would want to help with them. At least she could give me some pointers on how to deal with them.*

Mattie smiled. "Good. That's real good."

Josie looked from Mattie toward Gabe, as he left with the boys for the living room, and back again. Then she grinned and shook her head. Mattie had a crush on Gabe. Josie chuckled. She should probably warn him.

Smiling she stepped into the living room where Gabe was playing marbles with the boys. They were the only toys that Walt had.

"May I see you outside, please?"

"Certainly." He turned to Walt and Bobby. You boys stay right here and play with the marbles on the floor."

Once they were outside, Gabe wrapped his arms around her and brought her to him for a kiss.

She put her hands on his chest.

"What do you think you're doing?"

"I'm trying to kiss you, after all I won our bet."

"I'm trying to tell you something and you didn't win, we ran out of time."

"The time doesn't matter. I won Josie and you know it. What do you want to say to me? Tell me quick and then kiss me."

"Stop that." She was too aware of his muscles, his warm, hard body and needed to move back. "Mattie has a crush on you."

He stopped trying to kiss her but kept his arms loosely around her waist. At least she wasn't touching his body now.

Gabe cocked his head to one side. "What am I supposed to do about that?"

Josie shrugged. "I don't rightly know, but you should take care. I know if it were me, I would be easily hurt seeing you with another woman. Any woman."

He dropped his chin and stared at her. "I'm not stopping my endeavor to court you because of Mattie. You and I will be courting. At least we would be if you'd agree I won the fishing contest."

I'm seeing Gabe as more than just an irritating man. He's compassionate and caring about others. Look at the way he's taken to these children. Was I wrong about him? "Perhaps, but something is even more important right now."

42

"What's that?"

"They refuse to be separated." She sighed and closed her eyes for a moment. When she opened them she stepped back.

Gabe let her go.

"I can understand how they feel. If I had siblings I cared about I wouldn't want to be separated either." She paced in front of him. "And Walt is too old to be living with the brides."

He stood back with his arms crossed over his chest. "They'll just have to change their minds. Walt can stay with me, and the rest go to the dormitories or stay with you and your mother."

Josie stopped and stared at him. "You don't understand. Mattie would rather they live back in the hovel we found them in than to be torn apart. They need to stay together. Be raised together." *What I'm suggesting is extreme, but I don't see another answer for keeping them together.*

He frowned. "I can't raise them all by myself."

"I know." She took a deep breath and spat out what was on her mind. "But we could raise those kids together. I know this solution doesn't sound logical, but hear me out. They won't be parted. Period. Etta has bonded with you, so have the boys. They need someone they can count on. I could probably take them in with Mama and me, but we'd need a much bigger house and I don't want to take them away from you."

He cocked his head to one side and narrowed his eyes. "Tell me what you're saying, Josie. I don't want to guess and then get it wrong."

"I want us to get married, right away. You'll need to get trundle beds for the second bedroom and then add on to the house or build a bigger one."

"What makes you think I can afford all of that?"

"You're a Talbot. If you can afford to give Mama and me a house you can afford trundle beds."

Gabe stopped her pacing and reached into his pocket. He retrieved the small box he'd taken to carrying since the first night he met Josie. He was sure he'd be able to convince her to be his wife someday. He wouldn't give up until she said yes, so this was somewhat of a shock, but a good one.

"Very well." He got down on one knee. "Josie Long, would you do me the great honor of becoming my wife?"

He pulled the top off the box and took out a ruby and diamond band.

Josie stood, frozen in place.

"Josie? Honey?"

She took her gaze off the ring and looked at Gabe.

"Are you sure? I know I suggested it so we can keep the kids, but if you don't want this—"

He stood and took her in his arms so quickly she barely registered the change of his position.

Gabe stood back a bit and placed his palms on either side of her face before kissing her gently.

"I'm not letting you back out. I wanted you from the moment I saw you. And for you to say now that you'll marry me, when we've only known each other for such a short time, only proves to me that you want me, too."

"Gabe, you didn't let me finish. I want this to be in name only. A marriage of convenience. Don't read more to this than there is. I'm doing this for those kids who've had life even tougher than I did. At least I had Mama. They've had no one. They've survived for months by themselves and for the most part, did okay. They survived, but I want them to be children. I don't want Mattie to grow up and be like me. I want her to be a normal woman." Josie's voice dropped on the last words.

Gabe could tell she was thinking about her life and how hard it had been. She didn't want that for Mattie especially. Mattie was just about the same age as Josie when her stepfather disappeared and she had to take over his role. She saw herself in Mattie. He understood that, but he was too happy to let her back down. She needed him almost as much as he needed her, she just didn't realize it yet.

"I don't care why you're doing it as long as it gets us married. I figure I can woo you and I'm willing to take the chance that you'll never love me, never want a real marriage, because I know you will. I'm betting my life on it."

"There's something else I want you to do."

"What's that?"

"Hire a cook and housekeeper."

"Yes, we both lost or we both won, whichever way you want to look at it. I'm marrying you as soon as you wanted. So I should get the cook."

He put his finger on his chin. "Well, I suppose that's fair. All right, you get the cook. We'll have to see if we can find one. That might be hard in Seattle; women are scarce. Well, they used to be scarce."

"Oh, I bet one of those brides you brought would love to be our cook. She'd just come in every day, cook our meals, and clean our house, just to make some money."

"And what will you be doing each day instead of cooking and cleaning?"

"I intend to continue as I have. Hunting and fishing. Is that a problem?"

"In all honesty, I don't want my wife hunting and fishing. I'd like for you to learn to cook and keep house. For now, I'll ask my sisters-in-law if they can recommend someone."

"Thank you. Now I'll take that ring."

He grinned. "Oh you will, will you?"

She raised her chin and looked down at him through her eyelashes. "Yes. I will."

He slipped the ring on her finger, having to push just a little harder to get it over her knuckle. Then he stood.

"That's not coming off anytime soon."

"It's not supposed to. Your wedding ring should be worn at all times."

"I don't want to be wearing this when I skin and clean a deer or gut fish, but I guess I will."

"Or as I suggested, you could give up those things."

"Never. They are a part of me. If you can't accept that maybe we shouldn't get married after all...even for the kids."

"No. I'll find a way to deal with them."

Her stomach clenched and her breath caught as she looked at him through narrowed eyes. "Dealing with them is not the same as accepting them. Accepting me."

"I promise I'll work on accepting you as you are. It is just not the way I was raised. Jason, and our parents before him, raised us to protect women because they are weaker than men."

She squared her shoulders. "Your way of doing things is not the way I was raised. Anything a man can do, I can do. Better."

"It would appear we are at an impasse."

"Perhaps." She raised her hand to Gabe's jaw. "We haven't tried yet. We've only known each other for a week or so, really only a couple of days. We'll have lots of time to fight, or as Mama says to disagree. But that doesn't mean we can't work out our differing opinions if we try."

"You're pretty well spoken for someone who didn't go to school."

"Just because you found Mama and me in that cabin doesn't mean I didn't go to school. I went in Tacoma until Elias disappeared, then Mama continued my schooling as best she could in the cabin. If the tinker came by he always brought us a new book and would take back the one he'd given us before. He was a nice man, Mr. Bowd. He quit coming last year, and we figured he either died, or his company put him on a different route."

"He died. Here in Seattle. Heart failure."

She closed her eyes and said a prayer for Mr. Boyd. "I'm really sorry to hear that even though we figured it was something like that. Now just because I have some learning behind me doesn't mean I don't holler and cuss when I feel like it." Josie put her thumbs in her pockets and leaned back on the heels of her boots. "But, because of the kids, I'll make an extra effort to watch my speech."

"I'll try to remember and thank you for curbing your words."

"I'm just saying don't make me into something I'm not."

"I wouldn't think of it."

"Good. Let's go in and see how the kids are doing. We've left them alone for quite a while in a new environment. That is not well done of us."

When they entered the living room, Bobby was sitting on the sofa in nothing but a towel.

"Bobby, what are you doing? Why are you in a towel?" Josie walked toward him and sat by him on the sofa.

"None of the clothes fit me," said Bobby.

Josie turned her attention to Gabe. "Perhaps we'd better ask Mattie what they need."

"Fred Longmire is helping me. But the missus is the one who sells the clothes. She was unavailable before. He said he'd put together some other set of clothes when she gets back based on the kids ages as well as some groceries. I'll go pick them up now. She's been selling kids clothes to other parents for ages. I should have checked with her before. I'll take back the ones I got."

"That sounds good." She turned to Bobby. "I'm afraid you'll have to stay like that for a while. Sorry, kiddo."

"All right. I'll return what doesn't fit."

Josie went with Gabe into the kitchen. Walt was in the tub.

"Oh, excuse me." She stopped, her cheeks burning, and turned her back. "I came to see if you all had enough towels and washcloths."

"I'm fine," said Walt.

Mattie sat at the table bouncing Etta on her lap, with her back to Walt.

"I'll leave you and wait with Bobby in the living room."

Josie walked back to Bobby who sat on the sofa. He was too short for his legs to reach the floor, so his legs stuck straight out.

Nervous because she had no previous experience with children, she decided to try something that Bobby could teach her. She sat next to him on the sofa. "Would you like to play marbles while we wait for Gabe to return with your new clothes?"

"I'd rather you told me a story."

"A story? Me?"

He nodded rapidly. "Uh huh. You know a story. Don't all grown-ups know a story? Huh? Don't they?"

She lifted her shoulders. "I don't know. No one has ever called me a grown-up before. But I'll give it a shot. Once upon a time, there was a girl whose daddy died when she was little, and she had to learn to do all the things her daddy did, so her mama could keep being her mama."

"That's kinda like Mattie, huh?"

Josie nodded. "Yeah, kinda like Mattie. Well, this girl got real good at doing what her daddy used to, hunting and fishing. So good, that when her Prince Charming came along, she challenged him to a contest."

Bobby looked up at her, his eyes wide and full of excitement. "What kinda contest?"

"It was a fishing contest."

"Who won?"

She grinned and glanced down at her ring. "They both did."

Bobby frowned. "How could they both win?"

"Because they came across four beautiful children who needed a home. The girl and the prince decided they would get married and share their home with the kids. And they all lived happily ever after."

"That's like us. Are we gonna live happily ever after? Huh, Josie?"

"Gabe and I are going to do our best to see that we all do just that."

Bobby smiled and leaned up against her side. "Good. I'm glad?"

Josie put her arm around his shoulders. "Me, too."

"Me, three." Gabe stood, one shoulder leaning against the door jamb, hands in his pockets.

Her head whipped around toward the door. "Gabe. We didn't hear you come in. That was an awfully quick trip."

"It's only a couple of minutes with the buggy and they had everything all packaged up so I just had to load it into the buggy. I left the packages in the buggy. Would you help me unload, please?"

"Sure."

Josie stood and went over to Gabe.

"Her Prince Charming, huh?" He grinned.

She lifted an eyebrow. "Don't let your head swell. It wasn't you."

His grin didn't falter. "Uh huh. Not me."

Josie, feeling like she got caught with her hand in the cookie jar, jutted out her chin in defiance. "Maybe, not you. I'm seeing a new side of you, a caring, gentle side and not the happy-go-lucky not a care in the world type. I like this you. Let's get those clothes."

Gabe turned and walked outside with Josie following.

"Speaking of seeing a new side. Did you notice Bobby? He's a blond. Walt and Etta are, too. Just goes to show how much dirt and grime they were covered in. Let's get those parcels. Did Fred help you this time, too?"

"No, June Longmire, Fred's wife, picked out the clothes in lots of sizes that they thought might fit the boys. Baby Etta was easier. June and Fred have kids of their own and so were pretty good about having the right sizes for the baby. I bought two dresses for Mattie, one in blue calico and one in yellow cotton."

Josie turned her back while Gabe got Bobby dressed, and then he took clothes for Walt to the kitchen.

Suddenly Josie heard Mattie shriek. She ran to the kitchen and almost bumped into Gabe as he was exiting as fast as he could.

"Walt!" Gabe shouted. "We have clothes. Come to the living room."

"Okay," Walt shouted back.

He shoved a couple of packages wrapped in brown paper at her. "Here are Mattie's clothes. She's in the tub."

Josie entered the kitchen and saw Mattie washing her hair. The mass hung half-way down her back.

"Would you like me to rinse your hair?"

"Yes, please. Having a real bath feels like such a luxury. I can't remember the last time I had a hot bath."

"I know. I've bathed in enough rivers, creeks, ponds and lakes to appreciate the luxury of hot water and a real bathtub. If you'll stand, I'll pour this over you." Josie mixed water in a bucket until it was warm, not hot, and poured it slowly over Mattie.

"Your hair is much longer than I thought. And with the soap out of it appears to be red. Is that right?"

"Yes, I have red hair. What of it?" Mattie's hands fisted and she seemed to forget that she was naked in a tub.

I wonder why she's so defensive. "Nothing. I think it's wonderful. I simply couldn't tell what color it was before."

Mattie slumped a little and her hands relaxed. "I know. We all were so dirty. Thank you. My mama didn't raise me to be so impolite."

Josie handed the girl a towel.

"Gabe picked up more towels at the mercantile. Here's one for your hair." Then she handed her a second one. "For your body. New clothes are on the table for you. They should fit, but admittedly they won't be as loose as I thought they would be. You're old dress hid a lot of your curves."

"It was my mother's but it was the only thing that fit me anymore. Thank you. I see you're wearing a ring. Are you and Gabe getting married?"

"Yes, we are." *And I'm scared silly at the prospect of being Gabe's wife even if it is in name only.*

"When?"

"Tomorrow, if we can get the preacher to agree."

"You're doing that for us?"

"It's the only way we could think of to keep you all together. The boys are too big to live at the dormitory with the brides. They would have to live here, and you and Etta would go live with the brides. If Gabe and I get married, we can apply to adopt you and keep you all together, legally, although there is not a soul who would complain if we didn't formally adopt you, but Gabe and I want to do it right. Seeing as how you're fourteen, you can probably say 'no' for yourself but not for your siblings."

"What do you mean with the brides?" Mattie dried her body with the towel Josie gave her.

"Gabe and his brothers brought in one hundred women as brides for the lumberjacks and other men who need wives. They are referred to as the brides."

"So, Gabe would marry you just for us?"

"No. Gabe wanted to court me and we would probably be getting married, anyway. This just makes it sooner." *I'm lying to you and to me. I don't know if Gabe and I would be getting married very soon or at all. I'm marrying Gabe because I don't want you to be like me.*

The girl's shoulders slumped. "Oh."

"Mattie. I know you have a crush on Gabe, and I don't blame you. I have a crush on him, too. But I'll never admit it." As easily as he seemed to sneak up on her whether he meant to or not, she looked over her shoulder to make sure he wasn't anywhere near.

Mattie dried off her body and then pulled on her bloomers and chemise. Then she dropped the dress over her head and buttoned it up.

She grows much more and the buttons will bust on that dress.

"Why? You don't have to have just a crush on him. You can love him and that would be good. You're getting married, so he must love you back."

Josie sighed. "Things don't always work out that way. Just because we love someone doesn't mean they love us back."

Mattie squeezed the long strands of her hair in the towel. "I suppose not. What if you find someone else you love and want to marry more?"

"I won't. I'll tell you a secret, if you promise not to tell anyone."

"Okay."

"Even though I've only just met Gabe and I don't know him very well, I think I'm already in love with him. There's just something about him that makes me feel complete. I'm not sure how to describe it." Josie felt all warm inside when she thought of Gabe. But her mind told her that she didn't know him and these feelings she was having aren't real. "Mama told me that men get scared at the word 'love'."

"That seems kinda silly."

"It is, but she says that's the way of things. According to her, she didn't love my father when she married him. She knew she wanted to get away from her parents and marrying my dad was the way to do it. Mama didn't fall in love with Dad until Harvey was born and dad gave her a dozen roses for giving him a son. No one had ever treated her so well or been so attentive as my dad. She said a lot of little things added up to make her fall in love with him."

"But what if Gabe loves you, too?"

"Then we'd have the best possible marriage. One where we love and respect each other. But that is not to be. Now, shall we join the gentlemen and Etta?"

"Yes."

The two of them went into the living room and found Gabe sitting in one of the chairs, holding Etta, who stood on his lap and patted his cheeks. Her curly blonde hair in ringlets around her head.

Josie had never seen anything so sweet. She felt a warmth in her chest as her heart melted a bit. How could a man who let a baby pat his cheeks be bad? "I think she likes you." She'd come to stand next to him and was playing hide and seek with Etta.

"She just likes being clean and dry." His voice changed and he talked to Etta with a sing song rhythm. "Isn't that right, Etta? Yes. We like being clean and dry."

"I think we all do. Thank you," said Mattie as she sat on the sofa closest to Gabe. "I love my new dresses. I ain't never had two dresses before."

"None of us had more than the clothes on our backs," said Walt, a thin, lanky, boy with blond hair and blue eyes. He was on the floor playing marbles with Bobby. "Thank you."

"You're all very welcome," said Gabe. "Now, for sleeping arrangements. For tonight only, Mattie and Etta will take my bed. I'll sleep on the floor. Walt can sleep on the sofa base and we'll take the cushions from the sofa and put them on the floor for Bobby."

"What about tomorrow and going forward?" asked Mattie. She leaned on the arm of the sofa and stared at Gabe.

"Well, tomorrow, Josie and I will be getting married, and we'll be sleeping in my bed. Mattie will take the sofa with Etta, Walt will take my place on the floor and Bobby will stay on the cushions.

That arrangement will be just until we can get two sets of trundle beds in the other bedroom."

"Are you really sure you want to do this for us? I mean get married and spend all this money on giving us a home and food?" asked Mattie. "I know I sound ungrateful and I'm not. Truly, I'm more grateful than I can ever say or repay.

Gabe reached up and took Josie's hand.

"All Josie and I are doing is speeding things up a bit. Besides, don't think this is just for you. I wanted to get married right away anyway. But Josie wanted to be courted."

"And I still do. Just because we're married with children, doesn't mean you get out of bringing me candy and flowers and taking me for moonlight strolls. I read how ladies are supposed to be courted."

Gabe grinned. "Yes ma'am. Whatever you say."

Mattie looked at Josie and Gabe.

Josie knew from the frown on her face that the girl was not happy. What did that mean for Gabe and Josie? Trouble?

CHAPTER 4

Josie was glad they could go to the Inn for dinner. She had an excuse for not cooking then…there was no food in the house. The evening was entertaining as well when she and Gabe taught the children to play poker, with the cards Gabe got at the mercantile that day and using matchsticks for money. When it was time for bed, Gabe grabbed Josie's hand, but she shook it off.

"Mattie, will you get everyone ready for bed. I'll check on you all when I get back from Josie's."

"Sure Gabe."

"I'll be back after a bit, and I expect everyone to be in bed when I return. Okay?" asked Gabe.

"Okay," responded all the children.

"See you all tomorrow," said Josie as Gabe ushered her out the door.

As soon as they exited the stairs to the porch, Gabe took Josie's hand. He brought it to his lips and kissed the ring on her finger.

"Thank you for suggesting that you be my wife and help those kids."

"I was going to thank you for accepting my proposal. Taking on four kids won't be easy...for either of us. I learned a lot today and not just about raising children, though that was most of it. I also learned about family being more than blood. I care for those kids which surprises me given the short time we've known them. I watched them take on everything we threw at them today, in stride. I saw a side to you that I think I'd like to explore."

"No, raising them won't be easy, but after all that they have already been through, I can't let them be pulled apart by the courts in Olympia."

"I can't either. But I have something else we need to discuss?"

"What's that?"

"Our marriage. I want it to be in name only for the first few months while we get to know each other, just as we would have done while courting."

He stopped walking, turned and gazed at her. "Most couples don't really know each other until they get married anyway, no matter how long they've courted. But if you feel strongly about this, you can take as much time as you need. You always have the choice. Remember that. Do you want to seal the agreement with a kiss?"

She stopped and grinned at him. "Yes, I'd like that very much."

Excitement gripped her and her stomach was suddenly alive and rolling over in anticipation. Gabe didn't let her down. He turned her to him and cupped her face between his palms before lowering his head until his lips met hers. Soft at first as if he was getting the feel for her and then he moved his arms around her waist, pulled her closer and deepened the kiss. He bade her open her lips, and his tongue pressed forward, tasting her, urging her to taste him.

Josie had never been kissed like this, heck she'd never been kissed by anyone except Gabe and she very much liked kissing.

He eased back, resting his forehead against hers.

"I like the way you taste. I can still taste the coffee and apple pie we had for dessert."

"I like the way you taste, too," she admitted.

They walked on with his arm around her shoulder and hers around his waist the five minutes to her mother's house. She didn't even think of it as her house, she hadn't been there long enough.

She liked this. Being so close to him. Walking with their arms around each other. She liked the Gabe she saw today and knew her initial response to him was wrong. He was so much more than the cocky man she knew from their first meeting.

"What time are you picking me up in the morning?"

"We need to have breakfast before the ceremony, so the kids and I will pick you up at seven. Then we'll go eat and by the time we're done, Reverend Peabody should be ready for us. I told him it would be first thing."

"What time will your brothers meet us?"

"I'm going there after I check the kids and make sure they are all asleep or at least in bed. I'll have Jason and Rachel meet us at eight-thirty outside the church to stand as our witnesses. Hopefully by the time they arrive we'll be ready for the ceremony to begin. I think your mother should come with us to breakfast and then to the church."

"Okay. I'll tell her. I'm hoping she'll be happy to meet her new grandkids."

"Is there any reason she wouldn't be happy?"

"None I can think of, but Mama can be full of surprises."

They arrived at her mother's house and sat on the porch swing.

The door opened and Wilma looked out, holding a lantern.

"Is that you kids?"

"Yes, Mama. I'll be in in a minute."

"That's all right. Take your time."

Wilma went back inside, leaving them in the dark except for the light from the moon.

Gabe held her hand in his. "If anyone saw those kids when we brought them in, they won't believe they are the same children now. Who could have predicted that beneath all that dirt and grime were blonde-haired kids? Except for Mattie, and her red hair was a definite surprise."

Gabe tucked an errant strand of hair behind her ear. "You know, I've never wanted to marry anyone until you."

Josie dropped her arm to her side and looked at Gabe, tears pooling in her eyes. "I've never wanted to marry anyone before you, either. You make me want all those things I never thought about, children and happily-ever-after. But more than that, you make me believe they are possible."

"Josie, don't cry."

"I can't help it, you jackass." She was angry at the turn of events. She didn't want to change and yet she was. "You're turning me into a girl and I don't like it."

Gabe laughed. "Darlin' you are a girl and no one with a set of eyes can deny that."

She sniffled. "You know I don't own a dress. You'll be marrying me in my pants and shirt just like I am now. Does that bother you?"

"No. But someday, I'd like to see you in a dress."

"Someday, I might wear one for you." He made her want to be the kind of woman he wanted her to be and yet a part of her didn't want to change. She liked herself just the way she was.

Gabe took her hand and brought it to his lips. When he kissed the top and then the inside of her wrist again, she shivered and didn't worry that her hands were calloused and rough. They were working hands, but Gabe already knew that and seemed to accept the fact.

"Whether you wear a dress or pants or your birthday suit, I'm marrying you, Josie Long. Tomorrow. At nine o'clock in the morning. By nine-thirty, you'll be Josie Talbot, Mrs. Gabriel Talbot."

"I'm scared Gabe." Her stomach was filled with butterflies that seemed to all take flight at once. "I'm afraid I won't be me anymore, but just an extension of you."

"You'll always be you, but when we marry we are also an extension of each other. I've never been married, I was engaged once and I didn't think I'd ever want to marry."

"Why?"

"I'm not ready to tell you yet."

"I never thought I'd marry either. I've been betrayed by too many men to trust anyone. I'm still not completely sure I can trust you, but I want to help those kids. They touch a part of me that I didn't even know existed. I know that they are strangers and yet, I feel such a pull to them, I don't understand it."

"I do. I feel the same way. I wouldn't be marrying if not for them, even though I wanted to court you, I'm not sure we would ever have made it to marriage."

Josie wrapped her arms around her waist. "Given that we both feel like that how will we make this marriage work?"

"We'll just do the best we can and remember that the kids are what count in this."

"Agreed. Well, we should go in and tell Mama what's happening."

"Yes, I guess we should, but I'm kissing you again first...if you'll allow it."

She smiled up at him, though it was darker now, the moon behind some clouds, and he probably couldn't see it. "Thank you for giving me the choice."

He cupped her cheek. "As I said, you always have a choice, whether it's kissing or making love, the choice is always yours. Regardless of the fact that I will always want to kiss you and make love to you. You can say no and I will abide by that. If it's possible, I will never hurt you. I admit there are times that I'll kiss you spontaneously. Will you mind?"

"I don't mind. Once I get used to you, I'll probably like it. Most men wouldn't say that I had a choice, much less mean it. But you do, don't you?"

"I do. I'm not an animal taking a mate to rut with. I'm marrying you, a woman I want to share my life with. Have children with, even more than the ones we will have right off the bat." He rested his forehead against hers. "You're not sorry you're marrying me are you, Josie?"

She covered his hand that was on her face with her hand and leaned into his palm. "No. I'm not sorry. I'm happier than I ever thought I would be. Now kiss me and let's go in."

He covered her lips with his and the meeting was ferocious. He ravaged her, then slowed and calmed her, gentled his kiss and sipped from her. She didn't know what to think. Every kiss was different. She never knew what to expect and for someone who was just learning about kissing, it was difficult to keep track of all the differences.

He pulled back from her and then quickly kissed the tip of her nose.

"Let's go in and tell Wilma what's happening. She might even want to join us, for breakfast and a wedding, hmm."

Josie chuckled. "She might. What she will be is surprised."

They went inside, sat on the sofa in the living room and explained everything to Josie's mother.

"Well, I'm plum tickled." Wilma clapped her hands together and then rested them on the arms of the overstuffed chair. "I'll have grandkids to spoil right away and I know I'll have more coming in probably the next year or so."

"Mama!"

"What? Why can't I be happy and want more grandchildren. I wasn't blessed with more than you and Harvey, though it was not for a lack of trying on the part of your daddy and me. We both wanted lots of kids, being only children ourselves."

Josie knew she blushed from the grin she saw on Gabe's face and the squeeze he gave her knee.

"Look, sweet girl. The kids, as fast as I've come to care for them, are not the only reason we are marrying, it's the reason we are doing it so soon, but we were still getting married, kids or not."

She clasped her hands together in her lap. Knots filled her stomach. *Is this how I'll feel for the rest of my life? Anxious and scared?* "I'm just a bit nervous, that's all.

Gabe took her left hand, brought it to his lips and kissed her ring.

"I bought you this ring, hoping you'd say yes and you did. I'll do everything I can to be a good husband to you. Will you trust me?"

Josie gazed up at him and saw the earnestness and determination on his face. She nodded. "I trust you."

"Great. I'll see you in the morning. Get some sleep. I'll let myself out."

He stood, walked to the door, then turned and winked at her. Grinning, he left the house.

"Why are you so scared, Josie? Do you need me to tell you what happens between a man and a woman?"

"No." She fisted and unfisted her hands and looked at her lap. "I've seen animals mate. I have a good idea how it is all supposed to work."

"Then what's the problem, Ladybug?"

Mama doesn't often use my nickname. "I'm scared, Mama. I love Gabe, have from the first time he smiled at me. I know that doesn't seem possible, but it's true. I tried to put him off. I took that trip to Olympia, figuring that when I came back he'd have changed his mind. But he didn't. I tried again by making our courting a contest, but he won. Yet, I'm the one who asked him to marry me and he accepted but what if he never loves me back?"

Wilma moved to the sofa and put her arm around Josie's shoulders.

Josie rested her head on her mother's shoulder.

"Why would you think that he'll never love you? He's marrying you isn't he?"

"Yes, but that's for the kids, even though he maintains that we would have married anyway," she shook her head. "I'm not sure I can believe that." *It has to be. Gabe can't really mean he would have married me anyway. He's a man and though I will do my best to trust him, I've been hurt so many times by lies from Dad, Elias and Harvey.* "You know, those kids have had such a rough time of it. You wouldn't believe the condition we found them in. Mattie refuses to let them be separated even for one night. She said she'll take them back to the cabin where we found them rather than that."

"So you and Gabe made the decision to help these kids. I know you, you've always wanted siblings. Harvey doesn't count. He was so much older than you and he wasn't much of a brother or son for that matter. No you wanted brothers and sisters that you could play with and grow up with. Changing that yearning to children of your own isn't a big stretch. These youngsters stirred those longings in you."

"But what does Gabe see or need from them. He has brothers and now sisters-in-law. He has a nephew he's helped raise from the day that Billy was born. Why is he doing this?"

"My guess is because it's what you want and he wants you. I've never seen anyone so thunder struck as he was when he saw you."

"Me? I figure that's the way I felt when I saw him. He smiled at me and I just wanted to melt right there."

Wilma chuckled. "That's the way I felt about your father."

"But you married Elias. Did you love him, too?"

She nodded. "I did. I loved Elias in my own way. Not the same as I loved your dad, but I did love him. I was also very much alone. Even having you and Harvey around didn't alleviate my loneliness."

Josie looked up at her mother, eyebrows raised and eyes wide. "I never knew you were lonely."

"I'm a parent. I'm not supposed to show you my feelings of being alone or anything like that. I need to be strong for you."

"Mama, you don't ever have to be strong for me. I like knowing that you have the same feelings and fears that I do. That I'm not by myself in those feelings."

"Oh, you're not, Ladybug. You're definitely not. Gabe feels those things, too. Men like to be stoic and act all tough, but I can tell you from knowing your father and Elias, they have the same emotions that we do. They just don't allow themselves to show them in public."

"I think I'll go to bed now. Thanks for the talk. I think my nerves are more settled so I can go to sleep."

Wilma kissed Josie on the forehead and let her up from the sofa.

"I'm staying up for a while and reading, but I'll be ready to go to the Inn for breakfast at six-forty-five."

"Goodnight, Mama."

"Goodnight, Ladybug."

Josie awoke to a pounding on her door.

"Honey, get up. Ladybug. Come on get up."

What the hell? "Okay, I'm coming what's the big deal." She had tossed and turned all night and didn't feel rested at all.

"You have visitors."

Oh, my God, it's my wedding day! "Today!?" As soon as she realized what day it was, her hands started to shake and she began to sweat. Suddenly her sleepless night hit her between the eyes and she felt exhausted. *Stop it. I can handle this.*

"Come on out."

Josie opened her door in her nightgown and followed her mother to the living room. Rachel and Lucy Talbot, were there, each of them holding a dress.

Lucy stepped forward and took Josie by the hand, leading her to the sofa. "We know you don't have any dresses. We didn't want you getting married in your pants, so we brought you a couple to choose from."

Josie looked at the two beautiful dresses and started to cry. No one had ever been so kind to her as to care that she might want to be wed in a dress like any other bride.

"Oh, dear," said Wilma. "She hasn't had a dress to wear since she was about twelve."

"Look, Mama," said Josie through her tears. "One of them is even purple. It's my favorite color. I hope it will fit."

"We're all girls here, try it on," said Rachel. "You're about my size, I think, maybe a little bigger in the chest. The hips won't matter and the waist, well, I just let the waist out on this to accommodate my pregnancy."

"If it doesn't work, I'm sure this green velvet suit will," said Lucy.

Josie took off her nightgown and slipped the purple dress over her head. The bosom was a little strained but otherwise it fit well.

She grinned. "As long as I don't take any deep breaths we should be all right.

"I'm pulling your hair free from your braid and fastening it back with my hair combs," said Lucy.

Waves of hair rolled down her back to her waist when Lucy removed the braid.

"Beautiful," said Wilma, a break in her voice.

Josie snapped her head around to gaze at her mother.

"Mama? Are you all right?"

"Oh, yes, Ladybug." She sniffled and blinked back tears. "I'm terrific. I never expected to see my baby girl married much less in a dress. You look beautiful."

Josie gathered her mother in her arms and hugged her tight.

"I love you, Mama."

"I love you, too, Ladybug." Wilma pulled back. "Now let's get you married."

Josie took deep breaths and tried to quell the butterflies in her stomach. Why was it that ever since she met Gabe, her stomach had been twisted? And now that her wedding day was here the organ was in knots that were the worst yet.

She wasn't sure she could eat breakfast not to mention keep it down. Not today.

Chapter 5

When the knock came on the door, the older three women stood back and let Josie open the door. Gabe and the kids were on the porch.

"Are you…Josie? Is that you?"

She saw his eyes widen and his mouth drop open, heard the incredulous tone in Gabe's voice and thought he liked what he saw.

"Yes, it's me." She looked down at her feet. "Would you rather I put on my regular clothes?" She sighed and turned to go change. "Of course, you would. I look silly don't I?"

Gabe grabbed her arm. "You don't look silly. You look beautiful, I'm just not sure I want anyone else to see you this way. Especially any men. They'll be knocking each other down just to get a look at you."

"I'm sorry. I don't want—"

Gabe's lips descended on hers stopping whatever she might have said. He wrapped her tight in his arms and kissed her hard. When he broke the kiss he looked at her.

"Forgive me for kissing you, but I wanted you to know how I feel. Forgive me for not asking?"

"Yes. I don't want you to ask me every time you kiss me."

"Do you like the way you look? Do you feel good? Because I love the way you look and if you wanted to wear dresses everyday I'd get used to it. But if you are more comfortable in your pants, I'm fine with that, too."

"Well, let's see if I can get through breakfast and the wedding. Check with me later."

"You look real pretty, Josie," said Walt. "I remember Mama looking pretty like that."

"That's very sweet of you, Walt. I can think of no higher praise than to be compared to your mama."

Josie noticed that Mattie's mouth was in a straight line. Josie thought she must be angry that Josie was in a dress...and looked good in it. Perhaps she still had hope that Gabe might like her better than Josie, but when he kissed Josie like that...well, Josie could tell that Mattie didn't like it at all.

Josie tried to ignore the child, except Mattie wasn't a child. She was a young woman and having all the same feelings that Josie had, especially where

Gabe was concerned. This could be a problem with them all living in the same house or she and Mattie could try and be friends.

"Well," said Gabe. "Shall we all go have breakfast before this wedding?"

"Yes."

"Yes, sir"

Everyone responded, except Mattie and Etta. Mattie continued to stare at Josie and if the look in her eyes was daggers, Josie would be skewered.

After breakfast they all headed to the church. The day was beautiful and the steeple of the church stood white against the clear blue sky. The church was smaller than the one in Tacoma that Josie had attended occasionally when she was small, before her father moved them to Bridal Veil Mountain. Made of wood, painted white, with a tall steeple and a cross on the top of the steeple, it was a nice addition to the Seattle landscape.

Adam, Michael and Billy Talbot joined them inside the building. Drew and Jason who were with their wives Lucy and Rachel, respectively, came in with Gabe, Josie and the kids. They now sat in the pews with the rest of the Talbots.

"I'm so happy for the two of you," said Reverend Peabody to Gabe and Josie. "And for these lucky children as well."

"Can we get started, Reverend?" ask Gabe.

"Yes, yes. Now you and Josie stand here in front of me. Everyone else please be seated in the pews behind them."

When everyone was situated he began. "Dearly beloved, we are gathered here to witness the joining of this man and this woman in holy wedlock. If there be anyone here who wishes to give witness as to why these two should not marry, speak now or forever hold your peace."

Josie glanced at Mattie and could swear the girl wanted to say something but she slumped in the pew as she was holding Etta. She refused to sit and wanted down. Mattie didn't seem to care and let her go.

Etta toddled to Gabe and pulled on his pant leg, then raised her arms. "Up."

"'scuse me, Reverend," said Gabe as he bent to pick up the baby. "She's taken a shine to me."

"Ha!" laughed Josie. Then she whispered so only the reverend and Gabe could hear. "She's just like every other unmarried woman here and wants to be in my shoes."

Gabe grinned and whispered back. "What can I do? Female's love me."

Josie rolled her eyes. "Please continue, Reverend."

"Very well, where were we? Ah, yes. Do you, Gabriel James Talbot take Josephine Ruth Long to be your lawful wedded wife? To have and to hold, through sickness and in health, for richer and for poorer, until death do you part?"

"I do," said Gabe.

"Do," echoed Etta.

Josie chuckled along with everyone else including the Reverend. But when she looked over at Mattie, the girl still wore the same angry look. Not even her little sister's antics could make her smile.

Reverend Peabody spoke. "Do you have a ring?"

"Yes. I do." Gabe took a plain gold band from his vest pocket and put it on Josie's finger. This one fit a little better than that ruby ring.

"Good. Now do you Josephine Ruth Long take Gabriel James Talbot to be your lawfully wedded husband? Do you promise to give yourself unto him in sickness and in health, for richer and for poorer, to love, honor and obey him for the rest of your days until death do you part?"

"I do." Josie was excited to be taking this step in her life. One she'd never planned on. What she didn't like was the word *obey*, but she figured she'd just have to work around that word and it's execution in her marriage. She definitely wouldn't be obeying just for the sake of the vows.

"By the power vested in me by the Town of Seattle and by the Lord our God, I now pronounce you man and wife. You may kiss the bride."

Gabe leaned over to kiss Josie and Etta pushed Josie away.

Everyone laughed, including Mattie.

Josie gently took the baby from Gabe, handed her to Wilma and then wrapped her arms around Gabe's neck.

"I'm kissing my husband, regardless of whether Etta likes it or not."

Gabe chuckled and pulled her close. "I'm in total agreement."

Their lips met, and Josie would swear that it was the sweetest kiss he'd ever given her…almost like it was their very first kiss.

Gabe didn't release her after their kiss but turned to the crowd. "We'd appreciate it if you would be our guests and join us for cake and coffee at the Inn."

Everyone, including the reverend, walked over to the Seattle Inn.

After a half hour or so, Josie whispered in Gabe's ear. "I need to take this dress off and put on my own clothes."

"All right."

She saw the look of disappointment that crossed his face for just a moment.

Josie reached up and cupped his cheek. "The dress doesn't fit me right. One of these days I'll get one made just for me and then I'll wear it for you."

He turned his head and kissed her palm. "You don't have to do that."

She cocked her head. "I saw the disappointment in your eyes."

Gabe leaned into her hand. "I'm sorry. I'll do better next time."

Josie pulled back and gave him a watery smile as tears filled her eyes. "I thought we are supposed to feel happy."

He sighed. "We are."

"Then why do I feel like I just stepped on the dog's paw?"

Gabe wrapped his arms around her waist and brought her close. "It's my fault. I want you to be comfortable. Go change clothes. I promise to dance with you and we won't step on any dog's paw."

Josie couldn't shake the sense that Gabe was disappointed in her. He could say her clothing didn't matter all he wanted, but she knew it did. He wanted a normal, girly wife, but that wasn't her. She hurried back to her mother's house and put on her best clothes. The white silk shirt she'd saved for months to buy and a pair of black wool pants, were her clothes of choice. She examined herself in the mirror in her mother's room and thought she didn't look half bad. Josie left her hair down and the effect was, in her opinion, quite lovely.

She walked back to the Inn and the reception to celebrate their wedding.

Josie watched Gabe dance with Mattie. The girl glowed. Her smile could melt the coldest of hearts, but Josie was afraid Mattie's heart would be broken. Gabe didn't seem to understand that any attention he paid Mattie, just stoked the fire she had building for him.

Waiting until their dance was over and Mattie walked away, she went to Gabe and tapped him on the shoulder.

"Feel like dancing with your bride?"

He smiled wide and looked her up and down.

"You look spectacular."

"Thanks. I'm glad you think so. I've been saving this for a special occasion. I don't think any event could be more special than our wedding day." Her throat was tight, the words coming hard.

"True."

He leaned close and whispered, "Unless it's the day when I make you my wife in more than just name."

Josie felt the telltale heat rise to her cheeks and knew she blushed furiously.

"Stop that. People will know what you're talking about."

He chuckled. "They'd be surprised if I didn't talk to you about this topic."

She rolled her eyes and shook her head. "You are incorrigible."

"I try."

Josie laughed. She couldn't help it. She hoped he would always make her laugh throughout their marriage.

The party was winding down. People left to go to work, whether at the lumber camp, the mill or at home, cooking and cleaning. Saturday was not a day of rest, but a work day like any other.

They were out on the porch saying goodbye to the last of the guests.

Josie and Gabe stood side by side and accepted well wishes. When the last person had left, Josie put her arm around Gabe's waist. "Do you want to find out if there are a couple of lumberjacks who could help you build the trundle beds?"

"I've got two men in mind Lester Holden and Duke Jennings. They're furniture makers by trade and lumberjacks for the steady money."

"I'll see about getting cotton batting at the mercantile and ask if Lucy and Rachel want to help make mattresses for the bunks. I never learned to sew. If they can't help, I'll have to find someone to hire."

Gabe wrapped his arms around her waist and tried to kiss her.

She leaned back in his arms, knowing instinctively that he wouldn't let her fall.

"What are you doing?"

"Trying to kiss my wife."

She lightly placed her fingers on his lips. "We have work to do. We don't have time for kissing."

He kissed her fingers.

She giggled and removed her fingers.

"Darlin' we always have time for kissing."

She smiled and shook her head. "What am I to do with you?"

"Kiss me back is the obvious choice."

Josie pursed her lips, closed her eyes, and waited. And waited. Finally she opened her eyes again. Gabe was smiling.

"I thought you were supposed to kiss me?"

"I want you to keep your eyes open. I want to see your passion."

"What if I can't keep them open? I don't know how to kiss like that."

"We'll learn together."

He lowered his head and pressed his lips against hers. She watched his eyes darken and then she closed hers. She just felt. His tongue came out and ran along the seam of her mouth until she opened on an "Ah."

His tongue played with hers. She tasted him, tasting the chocolate cake and black coffee. "Mmm." She couldn't help the sounds she made.

Josie felt Gabe smile and opened her eyes to see him gazing at her, a twinkle in his eye.

He pulled back but the smile never left his face. "We'll have an interesting marriage, that I'm sure of."

She let go of him and stood on her own. "We need to get started on those beds. Go find your men and get to building. Oh, you should ask Mattie to take the kids back to the house and that we'll be there after a bit. She'll take that request better from you than me."

"All right. I'm going."

82

Josie walked over to where her sisters-in-law stood talking to each other.

"Lucy. Rachel. How would you like to help me make four mattresses for trundle beds. We're putting them in the second bedroom of Gabe's house so the kids will have someplace to sleep."

"Sure," said Rachel. "I've got a sewing machine and that will help it go much faster."

"Oh yes, that would be very helpful. I'm headed to the mercantile for supplies. Gabe has a credit line there. Apparently, all the Talbots do."

"I'm sure they do. Drew does and so does Jason," said Lucy. "Did you know there are empty beds in the dormitories where the bride has married? Those mattress pads are bigger than what you'll need. You could get two trundle bed size pads from one regular mattress."

"I'll go check with Fred for materials," said Josie. "How about we meet at your house in say an hour? I'll have to get Gabe's buggy for the cotton. It'll be too much for me to carry."

"I should say so," said Rachel. "Jason brought us down in the wagon. I have to get supplies. Let's get a couple of the extra mattresses and take them up to the house to be made into the trundle bed pads."

"Sounds good to me," said Josie.

When they got to the dormitory and looked at the beds, Josie wondered if instead of trundle beds they couldn't get these cots into the bedroom and put them in a "U" shape along the walls.

"Before we tear these apart, I think these beds will work by themselves. I'll go find Gabe and have him look."

She ran home and put a bridle on Storm and mounted him bareback. The day was gorgeous for a ride and she would have liked to kept going through the fragrant forest, but she was on a mission to get to Gabe. She caught up to him at the lumber camp. When she reached the office, she dismounted and tied the reins of Storm to the hitching rail. She walked to the door, knocked quickly and entered.

Adam Talbot sat at one of the five desks in a large room. One for each brother she surmised. Adam was like the other Talbot men. Tall, muscular and very handsome. He had brown hair that was liberally sprinkled with golden streaks from his work outside.

"Is Gabe here?"

"He's talking to a couple of the men out back." Adam pointed to the next room and the door to the outside.

Josie went out and ran into Gabe and the two men.

"Gabe. Gentlemen. I just found out that extra beds are in the dormitories. If we can have those, I think we can make them work and we'd only need three. Etta is too small to be sleeping by herself anyway. Before you gentlemen build us new beds, please let's look at those."

Gabe nodded. "Good idea. Gentlemen, I'll get back to you and let you know about the furniture."

"Okay," said the men and walked away.

They took the buggy to the dormitory after she hobbled Storm behind the office building.

They arrived at Dormitory Four where all the extra beds were. Gabe looked at them and measured them. Gabe and Josie went home, measured the bedroom and discovered that three beds would fit in the bedroom perfectly.

Gabe retrieved the buckboard from Jason's to relocate the beds to Gabe's house. The brides gave them the linens that went with the beds.

When Gabe and Josie arrived at home, Mattie and Walt helped them bring the beds in to the house, while Bobby kept Etta entertained.

Once they got the beds situated, Josie asked Mattie. "Do you know how to make a bed?"

"Yes."

"May I watch?"

Mattie shrugged and went about putting the bedding on each bed.

Josie watched carefully so she could learn. She'd never had to change the sheets on a bed. Her mother had always done that chore.

Gabe attached pegs to the wall above each bed so the children would have a place to put their clothes.

When they were done, the beds made, and their clothes on pegs, Gabe had the boys come in. Walt carried Etta.

"Well what do you all think? Will this arrangement work for now?"

Walt looked around the room and sat on the bed under the window. "I like it."

"Me, too," said Mattie as she claimed the bed by the door, across the room from the window.

The third bed was on the far wall and that is where Gabe wanted Bobby and Etta to sleep. Farthest away from the door.

"How come I gotta share with Etta?" complained Bobby.

"Because." Gabe ruffled Bobby's hair. "You're the smallest and you and Etta are both little enough to share one bed and still have plenty of room."

He turned to Josie. "Now we need to get you moved in."

"I packed my clothes in a valise last night. It's right by the door at Mama's."

"Shall we go get it?"

"Yes. Let's."

Gabe smiled at Mattie. "Please take care of your brothers and sister while we are gone."

Josie wrung her hands together and when they were out of earshot of the kids, she stopped walking.

Gabe turned to her. "Are you all right? Josie?"

"I'm fine but we haven't had a chance to talk about finances and I feel like I've been spending

86

your money rather freely today. That's probably because I think of you as a *Talbot.* One of those rich people who bought the mountain from Elias. I'm sorry."

"It's all right. If I don't have the money for something, I'll let you know. If you make any large purchases, I expect you and I to talk about it before the purchase is made."

He wrapped her in his arms. "Does that answer your questions?"

"Yes and I have another. Will you take the kids and I to lunch at the Inn when we get back? Cake and coffee doesn't make a very filling lunch."

He chuckled and kissed her forehead. "No, I don't suppose it does."

"And something else."

"What's that?"

"A cook and housekeeper. You need to hire someone. You may have won my hand in marriage, but I won the cook and housekeeper."

"Okay. I'll check into it."

"Sooner rather than later. Now let's go get my bag."

After Gabe and Josie returned to the house and Josie set her valise in Gabe's bedroom she asked Gabe. "Do you think you could take us all to lunch at the Inn. It's still our wedding day and kind of a special occasion. What do you say kids, are you hungry?"

"Yes, ma'am," was the resounding answer.

"I would be more than happy to take my new family to lunch at the Inn.

Mattie held Etta and was tight lipped. She didn't say much all morning. Just did as she was told.

Josie wasn't sure how to reach her. She was having a hard time trying to get any response from her other than a grunt or a shake of the head.

"Mattie, do you know how to cook?" asked Josie.

"Yeah." She shrugged. "So?"

Josie was trying really hard not to take umbrage with Mattie's attitude because she understood the girl's feelings. She asked sweetly. "So, will you teach me?"

Mattie narrowed her gaze. "You don't know how?"

Josie shook her head. "I never learned. I was too busy hunting, fishing, chopping wood, and doing the chores my father used to do."

That made Mattie smile. Apparently, the fact she could do something Josie couldn't delighted her. That was okay with Josie. As long as she found some way to reach Mattie, she'd do what she needed to do.

Right now she had other things on her mind. Her wedding night.

Chapter 6

Josie was terrified. The thought of making love with Gabe made her shake. Her throat was dry and her heart beat so fast she thought it would explode right out of her chest. Gabe had given her his word he wouldn't make love to her, but they would be sleeping together. What if he lost control? What if he…

No. Stop it, she told herself. She was borrowing trouble where none existed.

They put the children down together then went to their bedroom. It was her wedding night and she did her best to ignore Gabe and the fact that he was undressing. She pulled her flannel nightgown on over her clothes and then removed her clothes while still completely covered. When she was finished, she buttoned up the nightgown to her neck and lay on her side facing the wall.

When she felt the mattress sag and knew he was in bed with her, she turned over to face him.

"Josie?"

"Hmm."

"Come here." He held his arm over his head.

She lifted one shoulder and rested her head. "Gabe, you said we'd wait to make love."

"And we will. Until you're ready, but that doesn't mean I won't hold you in my arms when we're in bed. I want to feel your body next to mine, even if it is wrapped in that atrocious nightgown you're wearing."

"It is not atrocious. My gown is quite fashionable and new. Mama gave it to me this morning when I was packing my bag."

He cocked an eyebrow. "Remind me to have a little talk with Wilma."

"I'll do no such thing."

"Are you planning on making me raise my arm all night or will you come here and let me hold you."

She looked at him and her blood pumped faster. He was naked, at least from the waist up, but she figured from the waist down as well. He was amazing to look at. Wide shoulders, muscular chest, flat stomach and she knew he had long, powerfully built legs from the way his pants fit.

He was an amazing specimen of a man, and she was afraid all her resolve to get to know him before they were intimate would dissolve with his kisses and her new knowledge of his body.

Gabe patted the bed. "Come on. I promise not to bite."

She began scooting next to him.

"Unless you ask nicely."

Josie stopped in her tracks and glared at him.

He grinned in response and then broke into a laugh.

"You are so easy to rile up. I give you my word I will not do anything you don't ask me to." He suddenly got serious. "I'll always keep my word and I'll never lie to you, Josie. My word is my bond and without it, I have no honor. Do you understand?"

Her heart calmed and hearing his words she suddenly felt safe. Gabe would always keep her safe. "I give you the same promise and for the same reason. I'm an honorable woman."

"Then we understand each other."

"We do."

She scooted next to him and he wrapped his arm around her.

"This is nice," he said.

She lay beside him stiff as a board. He was suddenly too real. Too warm, too tempting.

He chuckled.

"You can relax, darlin'. I'm just embracing you. That's all."

She let out a breath she'd been holding and relaxed.

"Now isn't this nice?"

"Yes." She laid her head on his chest. "You smell good."

"Well, I'm glad you think so. I do strive to not be overly fragrant."

She turned just a little and laid her hand on his chest. It was covered with curly blond hair. "Gabe, now that we have the kids settled, we should apply to adopt them."

"Mattie may not want to belong to us."

Josie moved her hand and the hair curled around her fingers. It was silky and soft, not coarse as she expected it to be. "She may not want to belong to me, but I think she'd do anything for you."

"Do I hear some jealousy in your words."

"Perhaps. She's a young women, who fancies herself in love with you."

He covered Josie's hand with his trapping her fingers on his chest. "First, as far as I'm concerned, she is a child not a young woman. But I do realize that she considers herself nearly grown and many girls her age are married and some with children already or so I read happens in the slave states of the South."

"Well, she's certainly got the children. She's been raising those kids by herself probably since Etta was born. They say their father has only been gone a few months, but they were all so dirty I think it's been longer."

"You could be right. I also think you're right about adopting them as soon as possible. Every child should grow up knowing they belong. I never figured to get so attached to them so fast. Little Etta has me wrapped around her finger."

Josie chuckled. "Me, too. And I look at Mattie and, in some ways I see me. I had to grow up fast. I had to learn to hunt and fish in order to keep food in our stomachs. Mattie has had to learn the same things but she had even more responsibility than I did, having to care for her siblings."

"I want them to go to school. One of the brides, Mrs. Virginia Hall, is a teacher. She was widowed and became a bride, but she's agreed to open a school here. With Mattie, Walt and Bobby, the number of students will be at least seven, maybe more. I lost track of the children that are in Seattle now."

Josie could barely keep her eyes open. "We should go to sleep."

"I suppose. I'll need to plan a trip to Olympia and the courthouse. Find out what kind of paperwork we need to file."

"The sooner the better. We need to arrange for someone to stay with the kids when we go."

"Now that you're relaxed, I want to kiss you? Is that agreeable?"

Josie looked down a little embarrassed that she wanted to be kissed. "I'd like that, very much."

Gabe lifted her chin with one knuckle, then pressed his lips to hers.

Josie raised her arms, wrapped them around his neck and kissed him back.

Gabe rolled with her and brought her atop him, then broke the kiss.

Josie, surprised by the move, tightened her arms around his neck. *Is he losing control? No, he isn't. He is keeping his promise.*

"I like the feel of your body on mine. I can hardly wait to make love to you and really make you mine."

"I know. I feel the same way, but I still want my time...our time."

"I'll do my best to give it to us."

"That's all I ask."

Josie was up with the sun as usual. She let Gabe sleep while she dressed for the day. She knew how to make coffee, so she'd hope that the smell would awake the rest of the house and someone who could cook. What she really wanted to know is if Gabe had hired a cook.

The coffee did indeed wake the rest of the house.

Gabe came in, buttoning his shirt as he walked.

"Hmm. That smells good."

"What are we to do about breakfast?" asked Josie. "You said we could hire a cook and housekeeper. We need them sooner rather than later. I can go shoot a couple of rabbits for breakfast. But we still need someone to cook them."

Mattie walked into the kitchen holding Etta, followed by Walt and Bobby.

"I can cook. My mama taught me," said Mattie.

Gabe waved his arm toward Mattie. "There you see, Mattie can cook."

"I doubt that Mattie wants to be cooking every meal for us. Besides which she has to have the food available before she can cook it."

"I don't mind," said the girl. She glanced at Gabe and then lowered her gaze. "I'll do whatever you want me to do."

"Very well," said Josie. "Mattie can cook breakfast, but I want a cook and housekeeper for the rest of the day. I don't want Mattie to become our cook. She deserves to have a childhood."

"I don't mind. I like being needed."

"No." Josie stood up straighter and put her hands in her pockets before she strangled someone. "Gabe needs to abide by our agreement."

He gestured between them. "Our agreement was to get you a cook." Then he pointed at the girl. "Mattie wants to fill that role. Our agreement is fulfilled."

Josie pinched the skin between her brows and then looked at Gabe through narrowed eyes. "If that's the way you want to play it. I can do that. I'm going hunting. I'll be back in a couple of days." She turned away and headed to the bedroom to get her clothes.

He crossed his arms over his chest. "You're not going hunting. I forbid it."

Josie stopped in her tracks and turned very slowly toward Gabe. "I must have heard you incorrectly." She shot back, her voice getting louder with every word until she was almost shouting. "Did you say you forbid it?

Gabe had the good sense to blush, but didn't back down. "That's right. I forbid it and, according to our wedding vows you have to obey me."

"Don't you dare bring up our wedding vows. You're not abiding by our vows to keep me in sickness and health. Because you backing out of our agreement is making me sick and ruining my health."

She happened to look over at Mattie and saw the girl smiling. Josie had enough of Mattie's attitude.

"I wouldn't be smiling if I were you, Mattie. Just because you have a crush on Gabe doesn't mean he'll get rid of me for you."

Mattie turned bright red and no longer smiled. "I don't know what you're talking about. Gabe is much too old for me."

"That's right he is," replied Josie. She switched her gaze to Gabe. "I'm going. I'll be back in two days. You better have a cook and housekeeper hired or I'll move back with my mother."

"You're not going alone. I'll go with you and we can talk—"

"You have to work or watch the kids. Besides, we did our talking and you made a promise, which you've decided not to keep. Don't expect me to keep mine if you won't keep yours."

She went to the bedroom and picked up the saddlebags which she always kept packed, grabbed her rifle off of the gun rack in the living room that held Gabe's rifles, too. Then she walked out the door.

"Josie. Josie!" called Gabe after her.

She kept walking to Storm. She'd saddled him quickly and threw the saddlebags behind the saddle and tied them on. Then she swung up onto the seat and turned to Gabe.

"Two days. If you want to follow be my guest but stay out of my way, and make sure you get someone to stay with the children."

Gabe grabbed the horse's bridle.

"Don't leave, Josie. Let's talk about this situation."

Anger built in her. She couldn't believe that he was doing this. Was this the same man who had been so gentle and caring of her feelings last night? She certainly didn't feel like he was the same one. "If I stay, you'll have won. I won't let you take advantage of my good nature for a second time in one day. Goodbye, Gabe. If you care about our marriage, you'll keep your word and hire the cook and housekeeper. We talked about my continuing my work after we married, well think of this as my first time back to work."

Josie pulled the reins back and Gabe let the bridle go, dropping his hands to his sides.

"Don't worry, Gabe," said Mattie. "I'll take care of us. She doesn't have to come back here."

Gabe's eyes widened and his mouth opened but no words came out. He couldn't believe his ears. Josie was right. Mattie had a serious crush on him which he needed to nip in the bud.

"She'll be back and I intend to have someone hired. I need you to take care of your brothers and sisters, not the house. I'll return after a bit."

He saw the dejected look in her eyes. Josie was who he was thinking of and he left, headed for the dormitories. When he reached Dormitory One, he knocked on the door. Margaret Olsen answered.

"Mr. Talbot, what can I do for you?"

"Unless you know someone who wants to be my cook and housekeeper, I'm afraid you can't help. I'm actually here to see Karen Martell."

"I would love to come cook for you, Mr. Talbot. I am a good cook and keep a neat house."

"The position pays five dollars a week but doesn't include a room...yet."

Margaret smiled and her face lit up. "I'd like that very much."

"Great. If you'd come over in time to make the noon meal, I'd appreciate it."

"Certainly, Mr. Talbot."

"Call me Gabe, please."

"Very good. I shall be at your home at eleven o'clock. I assume you have something in mind for lunch."

"I'm afraid all I have is eggs and bacon. Before the children and Josie came I ate my meals at Jason's. If you'll give me a grocery list, I'll pick it up at the mercantile."

"If you'll give me a few minutes I'll give you a list for lunch and also for dinner."

"That would be wonderful."

Karen Martell came out to the porch where Gabe waited. "Margaret just told me the news. She's very excited and you won't regret hiring her. I thought I saw Josie ride out this morning."

Gabe took a deep breath and let it out with a long sigh. Then he ran his hand behind his neck. "She did. I'm afraid we had a bit of a disagreement this morning and she decided to go hunting for a few days."

"Days? I don't know much about hunting, but that seems a little long?"

"Depends on what you're hunting. For deer or elk, finding the animal can take several days."

"Are you going after her?"

He shook his head. "No, I don't want to leave the kids when we just moved them in. They need either Josie or me to be available at all times to feel secure."

"That's true. I'm very glad you recognize that. A lot of men who've not been fathers before wouldn't."

"Thanks. I had Billy to practice on."

Karen chuckled. "Yes, I guess you did."

"I have other errands to run. Talk to you later."

"Certainly. Goodbye."

"Bye."

Gabe rode to Jason's. He needed to talk to Rachel, Lucy, too, if she was available.

When he arrived, he looped his reins over the hitching rail in front of the house.

He found Rachel in the kitchen.

"Hi Rach, can I talk to you for a minute?"

"Sure." She wiped her hands on a dish towel. "Would you like a cup of coffee?"

"No, thanks. I need to get back quickly."

"Okay, what can I do for you?"

"I need some advice. Mattie has a big crush on me and resents Josie terribly. How do I let Mattie know that I'll never choose her over Josie?"

Rachel sighed. "That's a tough situation. Whatever you do will wound Mattie but I don't believe you can avoid it."

Gabe leaned against the sink and looked out the window at the mountain side. "I was afraid of that. The girl has been through so much, I hate to add to her grief, but it appears I can't do anything else. No matter what I do, she'll be hurt because I'm never giving up Josie."

Rachel cocked her head to one side. "Fallen in love with your wife, have you?"

He released a pent up breath. "No, don't be ridiculous. I can't feel anything like love for a woman. Not since Marian. I'm not about to let any woman do to me again what she did. My problem is I can't think of any woman I'd rather have then Josie. She means everything to me. But I don't want to love her or any woman. I don't want to feel the pain like I did when Marian left. I can't go through that."

"I don't know what happened with Marian, but whatever it was, was her problem not yours."

He hung his head and closed his eyes.

"I was engaged to marry Marian Harrison. I worked for her father and he thought the marriage would be the perfect way to have his company carry on. Marian didn't love me. On the night of our engagement party, she ran away to the abby and joined the wives of Christ. She became a nun rather than be my wife. What does that tell you about me?"

Rachel walked over to Gabe and put her arm on his back and then around his shoulders. "Absolutely nothing. It does tell me that Marian was an idiot. I doubt that Josie is. She seems like a very capable young woman, who unless I'm mistaken and I don't think I am, happens to be in love with her husband."

"Nah. We only married so we could take care of the children."

"That's a quite drastic solution."

Gabe turned away from the window and faced Rachel. "I think I'll take that coffee now."

"Of course. Sit." She pointed at the table and then went to the cupboard and retrieved a cup, which she filled and brought to the table.

Gabe rolled his head in circles to ease the tension. "What else could we have done? Mattie refuses to let anyone break them up and I'm afraid she'd take them and run away before letting them go to an orphanage in Olympia where Etta would get adopted and the older kids wouldn't. We can't have that."

"You and Josie are good people. Not too many couples would take on four children all at once."

"They are good kids. They deserve a chance. Josie and I both feel that way."

"You've got some tough times ahead."

The pit of his stomach churned. He placed his hand there to quell his nerves. "I know you're right and it scares me to death."

CHAPTER 7

Josie returned in two days, a deer carcass wrapped in oilcloth to keep the dirt and leaves off of it, strapped behind her saddle. She pulled Storm up in front of Gabe's house, no that's not right. The house was hers now, too.

She dismounted and dropped the reins on the ground. Storm was well trained and wouldn't move.

Untying the deer, she slid it down and onto her shoulder, bending at the knee so she'd be underneath the animal. Still the weight of the animal was great and upon straightening her back she had to take a moment to find her balance so she didn't topple over. They'd have to butcher the animal themselves, a process which she would admit she hated. With the kids here, having the butcher render the meat from the carcass just made more sense.

Speak of the devil, Gabe came out of the house and down the path to the road.

"I see you were successful on your hunt. Here, let me take that."

He lifted the animal easily from her shoulder.

"Thanks. That buck was almost too big for me. I had to field dress and skin it in order to get it on the horse. Normally I would cut the meat off the bones, but I'm hoping you'll let the butcher do it."

"Yes, I think that is the best idea. We normally cut up the meat ourselves, but it can be rather messy and with the kids here, I'd rather take it to Leland and let him do it."

"Great. Why don't you put the carcass back on my horse and I'll take it to him now?"

"All right." He placed the animal back behind her saddle and tied it on. "I'll expect you back in about twenty minutes. I have a surprise for you."

"I'm not sure I like surprises. I don't believe I've ever had one."

"You'll like this one. I promise."

She furrowed her brows and narrowed her gaze. "I hope you're right."

The smile never left Gabe's face, so he seemed pretty sure she'd like what he had for her.

She mounted and headed down the road to Seattle and the butcher. When she arrived she wrestled with the carcass and took it inside.

Leland rushed around the counter.

"Mrs. Talbot, let me get that for you."

"Thank you, Mr. Murray. I appreciate it. Gabe told me that you will butcher this for us."

"Oh, yes, ma'am. More than happy to. I keep a quarter of the meat to sell in exchange for the butchering."

"That sounds more than fair. Thank you."

"You're welcome. If you come back about this same time, the meat will be ready."

"Perfect. See you then." Josie mounted and went back home. She went directly to the barn. She was surprised to see a cow in one of the stalls and a chicken coop on the side of the building.

She unsaddled Storm, fed and watered him, then curried and brushed him. When she was done he looked to be one beautiful horse.

She smiled and patted his hind quarter. "You're one lucky horse. I hope you realize that."

He whinnied and bobbed his head up and down.

"Good boy. I thought you did."

She walked back to the house, smiling. Storm always put a smile on her face when he proved just how smart he really was.

Josie entered the house through the kitchen door, smells of food cooking assaulted her nose and a strange woman stood at the stove.

"Hi," said Josie. "Who are you?"

"I'm Margaret Olsen. I'm the cook and housekeeper. You must be Mrs. Talbot." She held out her hand. "Pleased to meet you."

Josie took the woman's outstretched hand in both of hers and shook it enthusiastically. *He kept his word.*

"Ah, I see you met your surprise. Like it?"

"Oh, Gabe." Josie closed the distance between them. "You kept your word after all."

She wrapped her arms around his neck and kissed him hard. "Thank you." She kissed him again.

With his arms around her waist, he kissed her back and when she would have ended the second kiss, he held her firm and kept his lips melded to hers. At first, she tensed, then she relaxed and returned his kiss.

He pulled back and then gave her a little quick kiss at the end.

"You're welcome. If I'd known, this would be my reward, I wouldn't have dawdled in hiring Margaret."

Josie suddenly remembered they were not alone in the kitchen.

"Oh, dear, forgive us for being so—"

Margaret raised her hand and shook her head. "Don't ever apologize for showing your love for each other. I'm a widow and I miss my Harold every day. If he was still here, you can bet I'd be kissing him every chance I got."

Josie kept her hand around Gabe's waist liking the feeling of being so close. Liking the fact that she could hug him in front of a stranger. "I'm so sorry about your husband. I hope you'll be able to find another man here to marry and to love."

Margaret reached up and put her hand on Josie's arm.

"From your lips to God's ear."

"So where are the children?"

"Mattie is in the living room playing with Etta and the boys are outside playing."

"Good. What are we having for lunch today? I'm starved."

"I have a nice stew, fresh hot bread and butter with a pie for dessert."

"Mmmm. That sounds wonderful. I better get cleaned up. Do you mind if I take a bath while you're cooking?"

"That's fine."

"Do you need some help with your bath?" asked Gabe.

"What? Oh, no. Thanks." *He was so quiet, I forgot he was here, too.*

"Darn. I'd hoped to scrub your back."

"Scrub my back?" Her voice was almost a squeak on the word 'back'.

He grinned and walked over to her while waggling his eyebrows. "Uh huh. Your back." He lowered his voice and whispered in her ear for her alone to here. "Your front, too if you want."

Josie chuckled. "You are a bad man, Gabriel Talbot. A very bad man."

"Only with you, my dear. Only with you."

She narrowed her eyes. "If you really want to help, you'll get the tub, while I put on more water to heat, get clean clothes and under garments."

"All right. I'll be right back."

He left the kitchen and went to get the tub from the barn.

"Margaret, I'm using the water you have already hot but I'll put on a couple of other buckets, if that is all right with you."

"That'll be fine."

Gabe returned carrying the bathtub.

"Where do you want this?"

Josie pointed to the corner by the peg board for coats. "In the corner out of Margaret's way. No way do I want to hamper the preparation of lunch."

He set the tub where she asked.

She got towels and a washcloth from the shelf in the pantry. Then she walked to their bedroom and retrieved clean clothes, her brush and comb. Arms full, she went back to the kitchen where Gabe waited and Margaret continued her preparation for lunch.

"What are you still doing here?" Josie asked Gabe.

"Just checking again to see if you want me to scrub your back." He grinned.

Slightly embarrassed, she stammered, "I...I'll pa...pass, for now. I just want to get this dead animal smell off me as quickly as possible."

"Okay. Call me when you want me to empty the tub and take it back to the barn."

She made shoving motions with her hands. "Will do. Now scoot."

"I know when I'm not wanted."

He gave Josie a quick kiss on the lips and left the room, to be with the kids in the living room for a while.

Josie stripped and climbed into the tub. The hot water felt wonderful on her tired muscles. Hunting always did that to her, at least if she was successful it did. Otherwise only her feet hurt from walking for miles looking for the elusive deer or elk. She rode Storm to her campsite, but she didn't use him for the actual hunting. That she did on foot. Usually she went after deer. They were smaller and she could handle them without having to quarter the animal to haul it back home.

She raised her knees and lay back in the tub letting the hot water cover her as much as possible. Then she closed her eyes and relaxed.

Josie awoke with at start. Strong arms were lifting her from the tub.

"Gabe? What are you doing here?" She crossed her arms over her breasts.

"Margaret had to go to the store and said you were still in the tub. I found you sleeping in the cold water. Are you trying to give yourself pneumonia?"

She put her arms around his neck and hugged him close to hide her body from his gaze. Being naked against his warm, hard body, was a new experience but her embarrassment of the situation prevented her from acknowledging anything further.

"I guess I was more tired than I thought. I still have to wash my hair. Since you've already seen me, and thoroughly embarrassed me, you could help me and make it easier and faster. But first you have to let me down."

He set her on her feet next to the tub.

She stepped back into the cold water.

"Could you get me a bucket of hot water and pour about half of it in here, please and then prepare the rest of the water to rinse me?"

"Sure."

He came back with a full bucket of hot water, poured half the bucket into the tub. Then added cold water to the bucket until it was just warm.

Josie mixed the hot water with the cold in the tub and then dunked her head before lathering it with the rose soap she'd brought from the bedroom.

Once she was done washing her hair, she stood.

"Pour the water over me, please."

Gabe slowly poured the water over her.

Josie worked the suds from her long hair. By the time the bucket was empty, she was free of soap. She wrapped her hair in one towel and dried her body with the other. Then she dressed in her chemise, bloomers, clean shirt and brown work pants. Lastly, she walked to the table and put on her socks and boots.

When she was done, she rolled up her sleeves and put her dirty clothes in the tub, taking advantage of the sudsy water. She added more hot water, and Gabe brought her a couple of soap chips. Josie scrubbed her clothes until she thought they were clean and then she wrung the water out of them as best she could.

"You can empty the tub now, but please bring it back in so I can rinse these."

"Certainly."

After she'd rinsed the clothes, she asked, "Do you have a clothes line?"

"Actually, I do. Surprised aren't you?"

"Yes, I am."

Gabe stood across the tub from her. "I wash my own clothes and it didn't make sense taking them back to the family house to do it. The line's out back. Let me get the clothes pins. I keep them in the drawer next to the back door. The clothes basket is on the back porch next to the wash tubs. You don't have to wash your clothing in the bathtub."

She shrugged. "Washing my clothes in the tub made sense. Why waste the water?"

"Did you have to go a long way to get water when you were in the cabin?"

Josie nodded, holding her arms extended so the still wet clothes were over the tub. "I did but rather than continue this conversation can we get these outside so I don't have to hold them dripping over the tub."

"Sorry about that."

He hurried to the door, grabbed the clothes pins from the drawer and held the screened door open.

Josie ran out hoping she didn't leave a stream of water across the floor from the soggy clothes in her hands.

Once outside, she slowed, walked to the line and laid the garments over it. Before she pinned each garment to the line, she wrung as much of the water out as was possible and then pinned them individually to dry.

"Okay. That's taken care of."

She began walking back into the house.

"How do the kids like Margaret?"

"They love her, except Etta. She's adopted me, I guess." He ran his hand around the back of his neck. "I've never had a baby adopt me before."

Josie smiled. She liked that the baby was sweet on him and that he didn't really know what to think about it. "How do you like it?"

He grinned. "I like it. I can't wait for us to have kids."

"I want them, too, but I'm not ready for...you know...that."

Gabe closed the distance between them and took her hands.

"Josie, I'm not trying to rush you, but I don't want you to put off making love forever. We've come to know each other pretty well in these couple of weeks. We've learned we'll make pretty decent parents and I want us to have that chance, sooner rather than later."

She sighed and released her hands from his. "We have children, right now. Four of them and if I never have anymore, I'll be happy with the ones we have. And if I get pregnant now, I'll never reach Mattie."

"Not true. You already know how to reach her. She's a lot like you. How would you have responded to someone in your position when you were her age, which hasn't been so long ago?"

"I don't know what I would have done, I didn't have that opportunity except maybe with the peddler, and I liked him just fine."

"How did you handle the peddler?"

"He was just interesting and I liked looking at what he had to sell. He was nice, too. He always stopped, even though he knew we probably wouldn't buy anything, and usually he left me a trinket of some kind whether we bought or not. Actually, I think he was sweet on Ma."

Gabe laughed.

"That's entirely possible. Your mother is a lovely woman. Looking at her I know what you'll look like at her age. Just like now…beautiful."

She rolled her eyes and tsked.

"Is that all you think of me? That I'm beautiful?"

He stopped by the tub and put his hands in his pockets.

"No. You're so much more than beautiful. You're smart, kind, and caring. You like to laugh and you care about other people's feelings. Look how you're worried about Mattie. Not too many women would have the determination to make friends with her that you do."

Josie's lips turned up into a small smile.

"You really think I'm all those things? And not one of them was good at fishing and hunting, which, by the way, I am."

"I know you are, but just like your beauty, your manly skills are there for all to see. These other things are what only those who are close to you get to see."

She frowned.

"If I'm all those things, why can't I get her to understand I'm not leaving and not giving you up?"

"Because she thinks she's in love with me and you are a threat to her."

"Well, I suppose in that sense I am."

He grinned and placed her hand through the crook of his elbow while they walked back to the house.

"I'm glad to hear that because I'm sure not giving you up."

"You're a nice man. No wonder Mattie has a crush on you."

"Does that mean you might like me a little, too?"

She chuckled. "Fishing for compliments are we? Well, yes, as a matter of fact, I do like you...a little. Now, what are we to do about Mattie?"

Chapter 8

Karen is right. Mattie has a terrible crush on me and she'll probably be hurt no matter what. I'm fifteen years too old for her what she needs is a man more her age. Maybe I'll play matchmaker. We have a new lumberjack working for us. Luke Jennings. And if Rachel and Lucy's reaction to him means anything, he must be good looking, too. I'll ask Josie if that might work.

Gabe walked out to the barn where he found Josie caring for Storm.

"There you are. I've been looking for you."

"What do you need?"

He walked over, took the curry comb from her and set it with the horse brush on the overturned bucket. Then he put his arms around her waist and brought her close.

"I need you."

Gabe melded his lips to hers for a sweet kiss that quickly turned sensual when she wrapped her arms around his neck.

He broke the kiss and leaned back, looking down at this lovely woman who was his wife. He realized he was a lucky man.

"I think I have a solution to the Mattie problem."

"What is that?"

"I want her to meet someone her own age...well closer to her age. I know of a young man who just started with the company. I believe he's around eighteen. I thought we could ask him to supper and see if they hit it off."

"Sounds like a good idea to me. When do you want him to come? We'll have to let Margaret know to make extra for supper and probably a lot extra. Lumberjacks seem to eat a great amount of food."

"Now why would you say that? You don't even cook so how would you know?"

She stepped out of his arms and gestured to her face. "I may not cook but I have eyes and I can see how much you eat. Heck, Walt eats almost as much as you because he's still growing. Is an eighteen-year-old man still growing?"

Gabe rubbed the back of his neck. "Probably."

"Then we'll definitely need more food. When did you want this dinner to happen?"

"As far as I'm concerned, the sooner the better."

"You go ask him to come tonight, and I'll tell Margaret to prepare for two extra people. That should do it, don't you think?"

Gabe shrugged. "I suppose so."

"Good. Now go find that young man."

She shooed him away with her hands.

"All right, I'm going. I'm going."

He left her and saddled Star for the ride to the lumber camp.

When he arrived he hobbled the horse in the grassy area behind the main building. This building held the office and some small supplies like hammers and wood chisels. Extra saws both the one man and two man variety, boot spikes, leather tree belts and other larger tools were kept in the supply shed, a building across the yard from the office.

He saw Luke coming out of the supply shed and couldn't believe his luck. The man carried a new saw and a leather tree strap.

"Luke." Gabe called out to the boy. "I need a minute."

The young man walked over. He wore no hat and his black hair glinted in the sunshine. When he got close, Gabe saw that he had deep blue eyes. His jaw was square and clean shaven, not even a little stubble. Maybe he's too young to grow whiskers, thought Gabe for a minute. No, he just doesn't have a heavy beard like Adam does.

"Hi, Mr. Talbot. What can I do for you?"

Gabe slapped him on the back.

"I'd like for you to come to supper at my house tonight. Six sharp."

Luke's eyes widened. "Sure. Thanks, Mr. Talbot."

Gabe smiled, happy his plan was coming together. "Call me, Gabe. My father was Mr. Talbot, not me."

"All right, Gabe, I'd be happy to and appreciate the invitation."

A knock sounded on the front door at precisely six o'clock.

Josie looked at Gabe and winked. "Mattie, would you answer the door, please?"

"Sure." She wiped her hands on a kitchen towel and headed toward the living room.

Gabe and Josie followed staying within the kitchen and watching from the doorway.

Mattie opened the door, looked up and stilled. Frozen in her tracks.

"Hi. I'm Luke Jennings. Is this the Talbot home?" asked Luke.

"Hmm." Mattie nodded her head. "Uh, yes, come in."

"Thanks."

Gabe and Josie came away from the door to the kitchen. Gabe went to Luke with his hand extended.

"Hi, Luke. Glad you could make it."

Luke didn't take his gaze off of Mattie. "Glad you invited me."

"This is my wife, Josie, and you met Mattie Devlin, one of our guests."

"Matilda," said Mattie. "Matilda Devlin."

Luke took her hand.

"Matilda. Pleased to meet you."

He finally released Mattie's hand and looked over at Josie, extending his hand. "Pleased to meet you, ma'am."

"Oh, please," said Josie, taking his hand and shaking it. "I'm much too young to be a ma'am. Just call me Josie."

"Yes ma'...er...Josie," said Luke. His gaze returned to Mattie.

Josie smiled. *Yes, this is working quite well. Let's hope it continues.*

"Come in now, supper is ready and on the table. The kids are already seated and waiting." Josie took Mattie by the hand and led her into the kitchen.

Gabe clasped Luke around the shoulders.

"We'll all get to know each other a little better over dinner."

They arrived in the kitchen and Josie and Mattie took their normal places, Mattie on Gabe's right and Josie at the opposite end of the table. Luke sat on Gabe's left, across from Mattie.

Josie liked this arrangement. She could see how these two young people were responding to each other. So far she had high hopes for a relationship to develop. They couldn't seem to take their eyes off of each other. Good. Very Good.

"Duke Jennings, made Etta's highchair. Are you related to Duke?" asked Josie.

"Yes, ma'a...I mean Josie. He's my cousin. He's the one who told me that Talbot Brothers Lumber was hiring."

Gabe introduced Luke to everyone else at the table.

One look at Walt's face and Josie knew he would be a problem when it came to Mattie. He wasn't ready to give up his big sister to anyone, regardless of how she felt.

Mattie kept giving Luke shy smiles.

So far, from what Josie could tell, Gabe's plan was working. As supper finished, Josie stood and began clearing the dishes.

Mattie grabbed hers and Luke's to take to the sink.

Gabe stood quickly and took the plates from her.

"Mattie...er...Matilda, why don't you sit with Luke on the swing for a spell and I'll help Josie with the dishes? Margaret has the youngsters corralled in the living room."

Mattie blushed but nodded.

"Come with me," she said to Luke. "We'll be on the front porch," she said to Gabe.

No mistaking it. She spoke only to Gabe never to Josie if she could avoid it. Regardless of how this situation with Luke resolved itself, Josie would need to have a long talk with Mattie about respect.

Gabe walked behind Josie, each of them carrying dishes to the sink.

Josie put the dishes on the counter and got out the dishpan from under the sink. "Thanks for helping me. I wondered how we'd let them have a little time alone."

Gabe put his dishes down next to hers and got out a dish towel. "I don't want to give them too much time alone. If I help you the sooner we'll be done and the sooner we can join them."

Josie put her hand on his arm. "If you're that worried about it, I'll finish here and you go join them."

"No, I want to give them some time. They need to get to know each other, just not too well."

Josie laughed. "That's not what you thought when you were courting me." Gabe had the good sense to keep his mouth shut.

They finished the dishes in about fifteen minutes. Margaret had put the pots and pans to soak before dinner and now they just needed to be wiped out and rinsed.

Josie dried her hands on the dish towel Gabe had used to dry the dishes.

"All right, I'm ready now."

"Good let's go."

He took her by the elbow and practically ran through the living room and out the door to the front porch.

"Well, how are you kids getting along?"

Gabe couldn't have said a worse thing to either of them.

"I'm not a kid, Gabe." Mattie's eyes widened and she gritted her teeth in a forced smile.

"Nor am I," said Luke as he stood to his full height. "I'd like permission to call on Miss Matilda. Do I have your permission?"

"The better person to ask would be, Mattie... er...Matilda," said Gabe.

Mattie beamed at him.

Josie smiled. Just like that Gabe had gone from possible husband material to father figure in Mattie's eyes.

"Yes," she said. "I'd like that very much, Luke."

Luke extended his hand to Gabe. "Thank you, sir, for everything."

Then he smiled at Mattie.

Josie thought she could easily have lost her heart to him if she hadn't already lost that particular organ to Gabe.

Luke's smile reached his eyes and showed straight, white teeth. His eyes crinkled at the corners and he had a dimple on the left side of his mouth. The man was an example of a lady-killer like she'd read about in some novel she didn't remember. He didn't even know it, or at least he didn't act like he did.

He held his hand out to Mattie and she grasped it. Luke bowed and kissed her hand.

"I'd like to see you tomorrow. Perhaps we could go for a walk down on the beach."

The two young people looked over at Gabe and he nodded his assent.

"Very well," said Mattie. "I'd like very much to walk with you. Shall we say seven o'clock, after suppertime?"

"That is agreeable. I'll take my leave of you now and see you tomorrow."

Luke walked off the porch.

When he was out of sight, Mattie threw her arms around Gabe's waist.

"Thank you, Gabe."

"Don't thank me yet. You need a chaperone and I can't think of a better one than Walt. So he will be going with you, at least these first few times. Hopefully, Luke can win him over like he has you."

Mattie looked at Josie.

"Is the chaperone her idea?"

"No, this is my idea and if you don't get that tone out of your voice when you refer to Josie, you'll have to do all your courting here at the house and that is not the best way to get to know someone."

Her chin rose. "But—"

"No buts. Josie is my wife and the only one I want. You will treat her with the respect she deserves. She's been nothing but kind to you, and you've rebuffed her at every step. Your snubs and verbal insults will stop. Now."

Josie smiled inside and fell in love with her husband a little more. This was the first time Gabe had defended her to Mattie. Up until now, he hadn't believed that Mattie was fixated on him. Now, he finally saw the way she treated Josie. And he would have none of it. Josie was so pleased. She could take care of herself, and she would still be having a talk with Mattie. But for Gabe to recognize the problem and do something about it, meant the world to her.

"Now, do you want to talk about Luke with us, Josie and me, or would you rather go to bed?"

Mattie looked down at her lap and then back up. Tears welled in her eyes.

Josie's throat clogged and she got sympathetic tears.

"I'd like to stay up."

She looked over at Josie who was leaning on the porch railing across from her.

"I'm sorry, Josie. I have been treating you badly and I'm sorry for that. I've been jealous and I'm ashamed of myself. I couldn't seem to help it."

Josie pushed off the rail and sat in the swing next to Mattie. She put an arm around Mattie's shoulders.

"It's all right. I've had a crush or two in my day." She really hadn't but Mattie didn't need to know that. In this case, Josie thought, a little white lie was acceptable. Neither Mattie, or Gabe, for that matter, needed to know Gabe was the only man Josie had ever had a crush on.

And she was feeling very tender toward her husband now. Two weeks hadn't quite passed, but Josie wanted to be Gabe's wife for real. She didn't want this marriage to be in name only, but a real one, for richer or poorer, in sickness and in health. She loved Gabe and it was time to show him.

"So Mattie," said Gabe. "What are your thoughts about Luke? I could tell that you were thunderstruck when you saw him. He is a nice-looking young man."

Josie looked at Gabe and rolled her eyes. "Don't be obtuse. He's a very handsome young man and if I wasn't married to you..." She looked at Mattie and winked.

Mattie giggled.

Gabe ran his hand around the back of his neck.

"I feel somewhat outnumbered here."

Josie jutted her chin at him. "And so you are. You have two love struck females on your hands."

Gabe narrowed his eyes and stared at Josie. "*Two* love struck females, huh."

Josie smiled and nodded, her stomach turning over at her admission. "Yes, two."

He lifted an eyebrow, but didn't say anything.

"What should I talk about when I'm with Luke?" Mattie put her index finger in her mouth and began to bite her fingernail.

Josie gently pulled Mattie's hand from her mouth.

"Talk about him and listen to what he says. Let him talk about his family. You know that Duke

Jennings is his cousin. Does he have any siblings? How many and what are their names? Are they married? Younger or older than he is?"

Josie turned in the swing so she faced Mattie as much as possible and crossed her legs with her right foot resting on her left knee and her right arm behind the swing back.

"You get the idea. And he'll want to know all those things about you, too, so be prepared."

"So many things to remember. What if I forget?" Josie laughed.

Mattie frowned and turned away.

"Honey, I'm not laughing at you, just that we all think the same thing. Simply let the conversation flow naturally. If you have a lull and want to fill it with something you can use one of those questions. You might decide it's fine just to be quiet with each other."

Gabe moved so he was directly in front of the swing and then leaned against the porch rail with his arms crossed over his chest.

"And with Walt along, you may not need to fill it with anything. He might do all the talking, so you can't. I'll tell you right now Walt doesn't want to give you up. He's jealous of Luke, much as you were jealous of Josie."

Mattie looked down into her lap.

Josie put her feet on the floor of the porch and placed her arm around Mattie's shoulders. "It's all right. We'll start building our relationship beginning now. What's past is past. Let it go. Now, it's time for bed. We'll see you in the morning."

Mattie stood, and so did Josie.

Suddenly Mattie wrapped her arms around Josie's waist and hugged her. Just as quickly, she let go and went into the house.

"Well," said Gabe. "Looks like you have a new friend."

"I hope so and I hope Luke doesn't break her heart."

"What would make you think he might?"

"This courtship is happening so fast. I know they were both hit with lightning bolts when they looked at each other. But what happens when they get to know each other and maybe don't like what they discover?"

Gabe shook his head. "I don't know."

"Neither do I. We'll just have to wait and see."

CHAPTER 9

Josie watched Mattie go into the house. When she was sure the girl was out of ear shot, she turned to Gabe and hugged him to her with her arms around his neck.

He responded just the way she wanted, wrapping his arms around her waist and pulling her flush with his body.

The door opened and the children came out dressed in their pajamas.

"We want to say goodnight," said Mattie.

Each of the kids got a hug from Gabe and a kiss on the forehead from Josie before they went back inside.

"Goodnight, my sweets," said Josie.

When they had gone inside, Josie wrapped her arms around Gabe's neck. "Now where were we?"

"I was about to say it seems a little early for bed, unless you had something else in mind, but I guess the time has gone quickly." He squeezed her close. "I don't want to make a mistake here, Josie."

Josie's heart beat speeded up and her blood raced through her veins. "There's no mistake. I want to be your wife fully. I want us to be a real family."

"Seems like I've waited forever to hear those words."

His lips crashed on hers.

He took all she had to give. No backing down, no gentle melding, this was a take-all kiss, a carnal kiss, where tongues mated, played, and shoved each other back and forward.

Gabe's hands went to the buttons on Josie's shirt and started to undo them.

Josie swatted his hands away. "Not here. Not now. Let's go inside."

He released a deep breath and dropped his arms to his sides. "You're right, of course."

Josie took Gabe's hand and led the way to their bedroom. She walked in and stopped in the middle, suddenly afraid of what was to come.

But she loved Gabe and he wouldn't hurt her. She had to remember that…he wouldn't hurt her.

She heard the click of the door, and then Gabe was behind her, his hands on her shoulders and then gently traveling the length of her arm and back up. He moved her braid and placed tiny kisses on her neck which made her shiver and goose bumps rise, though she wasn't cold, the opposite in fact. She'd never felt so hot in her life.

Josie felt him undo the leather thong from her braid and release the mass from its restraints. Then he spread his fingers through her thick tresses loosening the waves and sending them freefalling down her back.

"You have beautiful hair. I like it loose."

"Th…Thank you."

"Are you nervous, Josie?"

Her heart pounded so hard she was sure he could hear it, but she shrugged. "A little."

"It's just me here. I'm your husband and I care for you. I won't hurt you if I can help it, but I will tell you that this first time will have some pain. But never again. I promise."

She tensed and Gabe squeezed her shoulders a little and pulled her against him.

"Trust me, Josie."

She did trust him. He was unlike every other man she'd known in her life. He was honorable. Josie knew the basics of what was about to happen, but that didn't calm her.

"I trust you. I've seen animals do it. The sight of them mating was rather frightening."

He turned her in his arms and looked directly in her eyes.

"We are not animals in rut. We are two people, making love for the first time."

He leaned down and brushed her hair back to reveal easier access to her sensitive neck. He placed a kiss there.

"Yes," she whispered, afraid to spoil the spell he wove with normal speech.

He pulled her shirt from her pants and unfastened the first button, then the next and the next until the garment hung open revealing her chemise.

"Thank God, you don't wear a corset."

"I can't with the work I do."

He slipped the shirt back and down her shoulders until it fell, discarded, to the floor. Her chemise was sleeveless and he pulled that over her head, baring her to his gaze.

"You're beautiful. I knew you would be...perfect...for me and me alone."

He reached out, and a hand closed over her breast, squeezing very gently.

"Ahh," Josie moaned. She felt things she'd never felt before. Her body was alive, tingling and the excitement seemed to pool in the center of her being. "What are you doing to me?"

"Very little...yet. You are so passionate, I never hoped to find someone who would melt at my touch."

Tired of being the only one touched, she wanted to do the touching, too. She reached up and unfastened his shirt, slipped her hands underneath and shoved it off his impossibly broad shoulders, revealing his muscular chest lightly covered with curly blond hair, lighter than the hair on his head.

Unable to control herself, she ran her hands through the soft hair, feeling it curl around her fingers as though trying to make her stay.

Josie pulled back.

Gabe closed his hand around hers.

"Continue, please. Don't be afraid to touch me. I crave your touch more than you can ever imagine."

"You do?"

He smiled, placed her hand back on his chest and squeezed it.

She returned his smile and let her fingers explore the texture of his skin and the feel of his muscles as they flexed with each movement. Her breathing came faster and her blood raged through her veins.

"Josie. I want us to remove the rest of our clothes...together. Before I make you mine, I want to touch you and kiss you all over."

"All right. Together."

She stepped back, then undid her belt and the buttons before shoving the pants to the floor with her bloomers at the same time. She was naked as the day she was born and so was Gabe. He was magnificent. Lean and muscular, she doubted he had any fat on him. His stomach was flat, his legs long.

Suddenly Gabe scooped her into his arms.

"Oh!" The surprising action made her heart pump even harder. She loved the feel of his skin meeting hers. Pressing against her as he was, she could have swooned, but then she would have missed the incredible pleasure his touch brought.

He took her to the bed and set her in the middle of the mattress.

"Lay back and let me begin the loving."

Josie complied, her head supported by the pillow, her arms stiff at her sides.

Gabe chuckled and lay next to her, propped on his elbow.

"I can see some work is needed to make you comfortable. He leaned over and kissed her, took her mouth, used his tongue to taste her and bade her to return the motion. Her arms wrapped around him as much as possible until he was over her, braced on his elbows so their bodies touched.

It was a bit disconcerting but then he kissed her again and all thought left and the only thing that remained was feeling.

He moved to her neck, placed tiny kisses along the tender skin he found. Then his tongue left a trail of fire to her breast where he took a nipple into his mouth and sucked.

Josie didn't recognize the sound coming from her or the need that suddenly arose. She lifted herself and pushed her breast at Gabe, willing him to take her deeper into his mouth.

He pulled back with a soft 'pop' off her nipple and chuckled.

"You are so eager. Calm yourself, my sweet, I promise to take care of you.

And he did.

By the time he was done, she was a limp doll in his arms.

"Now, my dear, it's my turn."

Gabe covered her and made love to her.

The act was glorious, and the slight pain worth the wonderful feelings that came after when he sent her to the stars again.

Afterward they lay in each other's arms and she heard the deep breaths telling her that Gabe slept.

How can he sleep? She was awake and rearing to go. She wanted to talk about these new feelings. Did he have them? Would she always feel like this after they made love?

She had so many questions for him to answer...but he slept the sleep of babes and she hadn't the heart to awaken him.

With the dawn, the sun shown on the wall across from the bed, let in from the window above the bed. If by some chance she forgot what happened the night before, the tenderness in her nether regions would have reminded her, as would her nakedness. Her arm automatically covered her breasts, though she didn't know why since he'd seen and touched every part of her body. She shook her head and lowered her arm.

Gabe chuckled. "I knew you'd do that."

"You...you're awake?"

"I have been for a while. I was enjoying you cuddling next to me."

"I was cold. You were warm. Nothing more to it."

She knew if she could see him better he would be lifting an eyebrow and daring her to deny she'd enjoyed their activities the night before.

"Nothing more? All right if that is the way you want to do this."

He flung the covers off and rose from the bed in all his naked glory.

Would she ever get used to seeing him nude? Somehow, she didn't think so. She feared she would always be in awe that someone like him wanted her. Plain old Josie. She never thought of herself as beautiful, but for some reason Gabe thought her face with its chiseled features was attractive. That was all that mattered. Now, he was really her husband and as soon as they could get to Olympia they would file the paperwork to adopt the kids.

She didn't think a judge existed in the Washington Territory who would turn them down. No one wanted more kids in an orphanage than were already there.

Gabe dressed quickly and then had the audacity to lie back on the bed with his boots on and his hands behind his head to watch her put her clothes on. He grinned.

"What are you grinning at?" She went to the commode and wet a washcloth from the top drawer from the pitcher on top. Using the cloth, she washed the blood and seed from her thighs. Then she pulled on her bloomers and chemise, followed by her pants from yesterday and a clean shirt.

"I'm just enjoying watching my wife get dressed. I find the pastime most enjoyable."

She rolled her eyes and shook her head.

"You're a crazy man." She pulled on her boots and tied them, then rolled up the sleeves to the elbow. "I'll start the coffee, while you go milk the cow and then I'll gather the eggs. By the time I finish, Margaret should be here."

They went to the kitchen and Gabe walked out the door while Josie pumped water into the coffee pot. She lit the stove then set the pot on a burner and added about a half cup of coffee to the water.

She started to set the table for breakfast when a knock sounded at the front door.

Who would be knocking at this time of morning? Margaret usually just came in by the kitchen door without knocking.

Josie went into the living room and opened the door. A young woman with light brown hair and a tiny mole on her upper cheek, just below the outside of her right eye, stood on the porch. The beauty mark drew attention to her almond shaped, blue eyes.

"Hi Josie. I'm Roberta Egan and I'm here to let you know that Margaret won't be by today or probably the next few days. She's real sick, running a fever and Karen Martell doesn't want her working. She said Margaret needs to stay in bed."

"Thanks for letting me know, Roberta."

"Sure thing."

Josie closed the door and then leaned back against it.

Poor Margaret. What the heck are we supposed to do now? I guess we go out for breakfast and then I ask Mama to help.

Mattie approached Josie. "Who was that?"

"Roberta Egan, one of the brides, telling me that Margaret is very sick and won't be able to work for a while."

"Why does that upset you?"

"Because I feel bad for Margaret. No one wants to be sick, but I don't look forward to eating out three times a day."

Mattie laughed. "Why in the world would we eat out? I told you I know how to cook. Now would be a good time for me to teach you."

"I don't need to know how since you're here."

"Sure you do. What if this happens after I've already moved out...for whatever reason?"

Josie closed her eyes tighter if that was possible because she knew that Mattie was right. She took a deep breath and opened her eyes. "All right, where do we start?"

"You've got the coffee making, so next are the biscuits."

"Biscuits?" Josie squeaked out the words.

Mattie nodded her head and chuckled.

"Yes. Now we'll need flour, baking powder, salt…"

She went about gathering the ingredients and then showed Josie how to put them together.

Josie watched as Mattie mixed all of the ingredients together and quickly had a full pan of biscuits.

"That looks easy enough," said Josie with some trepidation. "What next?"

"Well, usually by this time I will have gathered the eggs. You need to wash each one and then crack all of them into a big bowl, beat them together with a fork and pour the liquid into a skillet. If we're having bacon then you want to start the meat frying before you scramble the eggs."

"Got it. But just in case you'll be here to help me, right?"

Mattie patted Josie on the shoulder.

"Yes, I'll be here to help."

Gabe walked in carrying a bucket of milk.

The boys came in from the living room with Walt carrying Etta.

Gabe set the bucket on the counter near the sink. "Where's Margaret?"

"Sick," said Josie. "Mattie has been showing me how to make breakfast." She handed Walt the egg basket after he put Etta in her highchair. "Walt if you'll gather the eggs instead of Mattie this morning, I'd appreciate it."

Walt took the basket and left for the barn.

Mattie went to the ice box and returned with a brown paper package tied with string.

"Let's get the bacon started."

"Okay. How hard can this be, right?"

"Cooking is not hard. You just have to pay attention to what you're doing otherwise things can burn or be too raw."

She pulled a package wrapped in brown paper from the ice box and uncovered the bacon. Mattie added the meat to a large cast iron skillet. She let it fry for a while and then turned it so the food cooked on the other side.

The bacon was done by the time Walt returned with the eggs.

Josie took the eggs and washed them.

Gabe strained the milk and poured the liquid into four quart jars, then placed those in the icebox. A quart and a half remained from yesterday, which he sat on the table.

Josie washed the eggs and then scrambled them before pouring them in a skillet.

When they were done she served everyone's plate and they sat down to eat.

"Thank you, Mattie," said Josie.

Mattie nodded, blushed and looked down at her plate before replying "You're welcome."

A knock sounded on the front door.

"I'll get it," said Gabe.

He put his napkin on the table next to his plate and left.

Gabe opened the door and faced a red-haired man wearing a black suit with a vest and a white shirt that had seen better days.

"May I help you?"

"You sure can. I'm Vincent Devlin and I understand you have my kids."

CHAPTER 10

Gabe stared at the man and realized he didn't look like he'd been in the wilderness all this time, perhaps injured. No, he appeared to be in quite good health, fairly clean, and definitely well fed.

"What do you want, Mr. Devlin? From the look of you, you're not here for your children, since you appear to have abandoned them to begin with."

Devlin scrunched his eyes and shook his head. "You don't understand about raising four kids on your own. You're rich though and want to adopt them. Is that right?"

"That's right, we were. But now that you're back, you probably want them yourself." Though sadness flowed through him at the thought of losing the children, Gabe knew Josie needed to know what was happening and what kind of man they would be sending the kids with. Gabe looked over his shoulder towards the kitchen and called out, "Josie, come to the door."

Josie arrived in short order. "What is the problem?"

"This is Mr. Devlin, the children's father and I think he wants his children back."

"Back?" She cocked her head to the side and stared at Devlin. "I thought he was dead and so did they, yet here he is in the peak of health."

Devlin raised his hands and shook them in front of him.

"No need to get ahead of ourselves here. I know you want the kids and I'm willing to let you have them for say, one hundred dollars...each."

Gabe narrowed his eyes and softened his voice.

"You're willing to sell me your children? Is that correct?"

"Right, but you don't have to make the transaction sound so bad. Living with you is the best thing for them and you know it."

Gabe stiffened his back and his hands formed fists. He wanted to beat this man to a pulp for abandoning those children and yet if he hadn't he and Josie wouldn't have gotten to know the kids, fallen in love with them or have married so quickly. "The best thing for those kids is a father who loves them and wants to care for them as he should, not one who would sell them to the first people to show an interest. Do the kids know you abandoned them?"

"Mattie probably does by now. She looked at me funny when I left to go hunting…probably because I didn't take food with me."

"That was kind of you." Gabe hoped Devlin would hear the sarcasm in his voice but the man seemed oblivious.

He hooked his thumbs in his vest pockets and rocked back on his heels.

"Yeah, I thought so."

Sick to his stomach, Gabe knew he couldn't let them go back to this man and probably be abandoned again. No. Returning them to their father wasn't an option.

"What if your kids don't want to go back to living in squalor? What if they don't want to go with you? Walt is very nearly old enough to decide for himself. Mattie would be if she wasn't a girl. If they don't want to leave with you, then none of them will go with you."

The man stopped rocking on his heels and narrowed his eyes. "You can't stop me if I want to take those kids, all of them. You see, Mattie will come with Etta. I know my daughter and she won't leave the little ones on their own."

Gabe braced his legs slightly apart and "Are you threatening me, Mr. Devlin?"

"It's not a threat Mr. Talbot, but a promise."

Gabe knew better than to tip his hand or make promises he couldn't or wouldn't keep, because in no way were those kids returning to live like they did before.

At that moment, Mattie came out of the kitchen carrying Etta and then the boys behind her. She stopped next to Josie.

"Father?" said Mattie. "What are you doing here? You're supposed to be dead. I prayed for it often enough," she added under her breath.

"Well, I heard some kids were brought into town and figured I should check to see if it was you. I'm glad you're here, now we can go home together."

Josie put her arm around Mattie's shoulders.

"No," said Mattie. "We are not going back to that...that sty, just to have you leave us again when you get tired of living like an animal."

Devlin took a step toward Mattie.

"Now you listen here, girl. You'll do what I say."

She lifted her chin and squared her shoulders.

"No. We won't. You can't make us. We'll all just run right back here if you make us go with you."

"Well, you're going with me...unless this man pays me like I want."

Mattie closed her eyes and slowly shook her head. "Don't pay him, Gabe."

Gabe nodded at Mattie. He was so proud of her. "I think you better leave, Devlin. If you want to bring the law to get your children, you should be aware everyone in town will know what you did. They'll know you deserted your kids and then tried to sell them. They'll watch out for you. You can't abandon these kids again."

Devlin took a couple of steps back and then turned back to Gabe. "Look, I don't want the kids. Why don't you just pay me the money then everyone is happy?"

Josie took a step forward. "Don't you get it? You can't sell your children. I suggest you get off this porch and away from here before Gabe throws you off."

Devlin stepped back from her and then raised his fist at Gabe.

"This situation isn't over Talbot. Not by a long shot."

The man turned and practically ran away from Gabe.

Gabe turned to his family and shut the door behind him.

"What will we do? He can take the children if he really wants to," said Josie.

Gabe looked at Josie. She kept her arm around Mattie as if to protect her and her eyebrows were furrowed and mouth turned down as if in frustration.

"No. That would cost him money and he doesn't really want the kids." He glanced at the children from Mattie's defiant face with her eyes narrowed as she watched her father run away, to Walt's worried look. "Devlin just wants the money he thinks we'll pay for them," replied Gabe.

"What happens to us when you don't pay?" asked Mattie.

"Nothing. You're staying right where you are." Gabe moved to the closest window watched Devlin walk toward town. No doubt he was headed to the saloon to drown his sorrows or to give him courage for something else. What that something else was, Gabe didn't know, but he'd be on his guard for anything from Vincent Devlin.

Gabe and Josie packed up the kids and left them with Jason. He knew Jason would protect the kids from their father while Gabe and Josie rode hard to Olympia to file for adoption of the children due to abandonment by their father. The sooner they got legal custody of the kids the sooner he could tell Devlin to go to hell.

A week after they returned from Olympia, Gabe returned to work. He couldn't stay home with Josie and the kids forever. Josie knew this but knowing he had to work didn't stop her from wanting him to stay.

He hadn't been gone an hour when a knock sounded on the front door.

"I'll get it," called Mattie who had just picked Etta up from the living room floor.

Josie ran for the door afraid she already knew who was on the other side. "No, let me—"

She watched Mattie open the door to a grinning Vincent Devlin.

"Hi, Mattie, girl. Why don't you let your father in? I've got some talkin' to do with the missus."

"Why can't you just go away and leave us for good. We're better off now than we ever were with you. Safer, too. Just leave us alone." Mattie shouted those last words. She tried to shoulder the door closed but couldn't with Etta in her arms.

"Afraid I can't do that little girl. Yer new family has somethin' I need. Money."

He pushed Mattie aside, knocking her down, and stepped into the house. Mattie protected Etta as she fell and made sure the baby didn't get hurt.

Josie ran forward and helped Mattie and Etta rise. Panicked, afraid he'd try to take the children, she put herself between the kids and Devlin.

"Get out of my house, Mr. Devlin. You're not welcome here."

"Out of my way, girlie." He slapped Josie in the face and she turned her head and gave him a fist in the jaw. He fell back but caught himself.

"You want to get in my way, I'll make sure you can't get up." He hit her in the stomach with his right fist and followed by a left to her jaw.

She fell cracking the side of her face on the floor. He loomed over her, grinned and then kicked her in the side. "I'm taking my kids and leaving. I'm taking them back to the cabin you found them in. If you want them back, you'll bring my money."

Mattie gave a crying Etta to Walt and ran to Josie. "I'm so sorry. So very sorry."

She looked over at her father.

"We'll go with you. Just don't hurt her anymore."

"I'll leave her alone. She's got to tell that husband of hers what's what now, don't she?"

Mattie took Etta from Walt and tried to soothe her.

Walt stood staring at his father, his hands in fists at his sides.

Bobby stood wide-eyed, peeking around Walt.

"Let's go. I've got a wagon out here. Get in it and don't make me have to beat you."

The children followed him out, but Maddie looked over her shoulder at Josie.

"I'm so sorry, Josie. So very sorry."

Then the door shut and she was alone.

Josie held her throbbing face where Devlin had hit her. Her ribs hurt and she had trouble breathing. Her vision was blurry as she watched the kids follow their father out of the door.

She had to get Gabe. No, she had to stop Devlin. Josie stood and took a couple of steps toward the gun rack. She couldn't see straight and when she stood she felt dizzy. She couldn't shoot at Devlin, she might hit one of the kids.

Placing her hands on her jaws, she closed her eyes and lay back on the sofa. She needed to rest a minute, perhaps then her vision would return and could stand without falling.

She awoke in the dark, her ribs hurt like crazy and she had trouble breathing without pain.

Gabe held a lamp over her.

"Josie? What happened? Where are the kids?"

She burst into tears.

"I tried to stop him. I tried to keep him from taking them, but he hit me and I hit him back, a good one in the jaw, but the blow didn't take him down. He hit me in the stomach and then again in my jaw. When I fell to the floor, he kicked me in the ribs. When I got up to get the gun and shoot him, I couldn't see. My vision was too blurry and I was so dizzy. I was afraid I'd hit one of the kids."

Gabe sat on the couch next to her prone body with the kerosene lamp held aloft.

The light hurt Josie's eyes and she lifted her hand until she blocked the light from reaching her.

"Sorry." Gabe put the lamp on the table. "Now, tell me exactly what happened."

She told him all the terrible things that happened.

"I just wanted to lie down long enough for my vision to clear so I could go after him. He was in a wagon. I could easily have overtaken him on Storm."

"Are you feeling better now? Do you want Karen Martell to look you over?"

"No. I'm fine."

Gabe sat on the table in front of the sofa. "What did Devlin say to you? Anything?"

All kinds of scenarios ran though Josie's head of things Devlin could be doing to the children. He'd threatened to beat them if they didn't do what he said. She was terrified he would hurt them, taking out his frustration at Gabe's refusal on them.

She nodded and moaned. "Ahh. Remind me not to move my head. He said he was taking them to their cabin and if we wanted them back to bring his money."

"I want Karen to look you over. You were unconscious for too long and I want her to make sure nothing is broken." He gently touched her face. "I'll make him pay for what he did to you. And we'll get our kids back. After you see Karen, we'll go to Jason's."

"You're paying him?"

He frowned and Josie saw the anger in his gaze. "No, we're not paying him. We're not buying the children. But if he wants to live, he'll relinquish the kids. We've already seen the place and know the one door and that tiny window are the only openings. It will be dark but we'll still have to come in on the backside...well my brothers will have to come in on the backside, out of sight, to take the rifle like I did with Mattie.

"Why can't I do that?"

"Because he'll want to see you and me. He won't expect my brothers will be ready to breach the door as soon as he's occupied by us. Trust me."

Josie sat up, her head pounded unlike anything she'd ever experienced, but she knew she had to move, to prove to Gabe she could travel. She wrapped her arms around Gabe. "I do trust you and you've never steered me wrong."

Gabe returned her hug, but gently.

She could tell he didn't want to hurt her and, since everything hurt, she was especially thankful for his restraint.

"Are you ready to go see Karen? Can you walk or do you need me to get the buggy?"

She laughed and then grimaced. "Please don't make me laugh, it hurts like hell. I'm fully capable of walking, he only hit me in the face and kicked me once in the side. That was what caused the children to go with him." She frowned at the memory and liquid filled her eyes so she couldn't see. "They were protecting me, when they should have run."

"Shh. We'll get the kids back."

She laid her head against his broad chest and let the tears fall, running in a silent stream down her cheeks.

After a few minutes she sat back and wiped her wet face with the palms of her hands. "All right, I'm ready now and I won't give him the satisfaction of seeing me down, but we should probably take the buggy. We can go directly from Karen's to Jason's that way."

Gabe took her hand and, together, they walked to the barn. She sat on the milking stool while Gabe hitched Buttons to the buggy.

"All right. Let's go."

He helped her into the buggy and they headed for Dormitory One.

When they got to the building Karen's young son, Larry, opened the door.

Gabe knelt down to the child's height. "Hi, Larry. Are you supposed to be answering the door?"

Larry nodded vigorously. "Mama's puttin' my sister to bed and said I could answer the knock 'cause all the other ladies are gone."

"As long as your mama knows. We need to see your mama. Do you think you could tell her we're here?"

"Okay. Be right back."

A minute or so later, Karen appeared at the door.

Josie saw that Karen was upset, her eyes were narrow and her mouth downturned.

"I'm sorry Karen. We can come back at another time."

She shook her head and smiled.

"Nonsense and just look at you. Come into the kitchen where I can see better. What in the world happened?"

Gabe helped Josie to the kitchen, while she told Karen her story as they walked.

"Sit on the table please and I'll see if any of your ribs are broken. I can't do anything about your face and I'm pretty sure your jaw isn't broken because you are talking."

Josie sat as instructed. She winced when she got on the table. Her ribs did not like that particular movement.

Karen stood in front of her.

"Which side did he kick you on?"

"The right."

Karen ran her fingers over and pressed on Josie's right side, up and down her ribcage a couple of times.

"Well, I think you may have a couple of bruised ribs but nothing appears to be broken. You need to take it easy for a few days. You won't feel like doing much of anything anyway because you'll be sore when the shock to your system wears off."

"It's already worn off. I ache all over, not just my side."

"That's all right. You'll feel better in a couple of days. In the meantime, take a little laudanum. Five drops in a glass of water should help." Karen turned toward Gabe who leaned against the counter. "Gabe, do you have laudanum at home?"

"Yes, I do. I'll make sure she takes it and gets a good night's rest."

Josie looked at him and cocked an eyebrow in question.

"Good. If you aren't feeling better in a few days come back and I'll check you again to see if I missed something."

Josie nodded. "Thanks, Karen. Say, when will you open your own practice? You're the closest thing to a doctor we have and you should be getting paid for your services. How much do we owe you?"

"Nothing. If you want have us up for supper sometime. I'd like for Larry and Patty to meet your kids."

Tears burned behind Josie's eyes as she thought of the kids. She looked over at Gabe.

He frowned.

"We'll do that very soon."

Karen laid her hand on Josie's leg. "I hope you get the children back quickly."

"Oh, we will and the reprobate who says he's their father will pay for what he did to Josie and those kids."

Gabe's voice was so low when he spoke, Josie could barely hear him. The quieter he got the angrier he was. Right now she was sure killing Vincent Devlin was all he wanted to do.

And Josie wasn't sure she'd stop him if he tried.

CHAPTER 11

They dropped the buggy off at the house and Gabe saddled both Star and Storm. Then he help Josie into the saddle. She had a hard time moving because of her bruised ribs but she was determined to get the kids back.

When they arrived at Jason's they left their horses out front tied to the hitching rail, ready to go at a moment's notice.

The hour was about nine o'clock at night. Everyone except Billy was in the living room, playing cards or reading.

His brothers and his sisters-in-law all looked up when Gabe and Josie walked in.

Jason set his cards on the table.

"Gabe, Josie—good Lord, Josie! What happened to you?" He stood and walked over to them where he took Josie by the hand and escorted her to the kitchen.

"Here take a seat. Have you eaten? We had plenty left over from supper."

He turned to Rachel. "Sweetheart, would you get Josie and Gabe plates, please?"

"No, we're not hungry. We need your help."

"Of course, but first I need a hug from my brother and sister-in-law."

She hugged Josie, very gently, first. "Are you all right? Did you see Karen?"

"Yes," answered Josie. "Gabe took me to see her, against my protests, earlier tonight."

"Good, now sit and at least let me get you a cup of coffee."

Then Rachel turned to Gabe and held her arms wide.

Gabe wrapped her in his arms and gave her a bear hug.

"Now," she said, letting go of Gabe. "Sit in my seat next to Josie and I'll get you a cup, too."

Gabe gave her a kiss on the cheek. "Thanks, Rachel."

When Josie and Gabe were seated, Drew, his baby brother, said, "Tell us what happened and who we have to kill."

Gabe narrowed his eyes and the skin between his brows creased. "The only killing to be done will be by me when I catch the—"

Josie kicked him under the table. "Language. Ladies are present."

Gabe nodded. "When I catch the children's father, I intend to make him pay for what he did to Josie and to his own blood. He left those children to die. He had no way of knowing that they would be able to fend for themselves as they did. They are amazing."

"You're more generous that I would be," said Drew. "I'd kill the son-of-a-bitch."

Lucy nodded. "I understand the emotion. If I could have killed Harvey any sooner, I would have. I could have saved myself a lot of pain. I'm sorry Josie, I know he was your brother —"

"Don't apologize to me. If I could have killed him for you I would have."

Lucy smiled.

She and I are the closest, because of my brother Harvey, who abused us both, though in different ways. But none of that mattered now. Because of Lucy, I met Gabe and we are married, for richer or poorer.

Gabe snapped his fingers in front of Josie's face.

She shook her head to clear it and concentrated on what Gabe was saying.

"What?"

"I need to tell them the plan," said Gabe. "I'm sure they'll agree that both of us need to be out front for Devlin to see, and I need to carry saddle bags as though we are bringing him the money for the kids."

Josie ate as much as she could, which amounted to a little bread and coffee. If she ate any more she was afraid she'd throw up.

Gabe noticed how little Josie ate. "Are you all right? You didn't eat much."

"I'm not hungry. Too much excitement probably."

"Okay, but when we get the kids back, you're lying down and resting. No cooking lessons or anything else."

"All right. I won't argue. I hurt too much for that. When are we getting this show on the road?" asked Josie.

"You're rather anxious, don't you think?" asked Gabe.

"I just want this over with and to get the kids back as soon as possible."

Gabe covered her hand with his. "I understand that, but we have to explain the situation to them and form a plan."

"So tell us, what is the situation?" asked Jason.

Gabe explained everything that happened.

"What I want you four to do is come around the back of the house and stand to the sides of the door and the window. When Devlin sticks his gun out the window, I want you to take it from him and then break down the door and get back our children."

Michael, the renegade brother because he dressed like a cowboy, stood. He walked to the coat-rack, plucked his gun belt from one of the pegs and put it on.

"We know enough. Let's go get your kids."

Josie almost burst into tears when one-by-one her brothers-in-law stood and walked toward the door. She remembered when she was about sixteen and had nearly been assaulted by one of the Walker boys in Tacoma. She hadn't had anyone to help her that day, no brothers-in-law to help her. Luckily, their mother came out and broke up the situation. She didn't go to Tacoma unarmed after that and she steered clear of the Walkers.

Drew looked back over his shoulder. "Are you two coming or you sitting at the kitchen table all night?"

Josie laughed, then moaned and pressed a hand to her side. "I'm coming. Our horses are already to go. We'll meet you at the barn."

Rachel and Lucy both went to the door with their husbands and kissed them goodbye.

"Be safe," said Rachel.

Jason wrapped his arms around his wife.

"I intend to. I've got you here waiting for me."

He kissed her passionately.

"Okay, you two, let's get going," said Adam.

Jason and Rachel broke apart and Jason went out the door.

Drew was holding Lucy.

"Please be careful." She cupped his cheek with her hand. "This man sounds desperate. He could do anything if he could take his own kids and hold them for ransom."

"I'll be careful. You stay here with Rachel and Billy."

"I will. We'll be safe, don't worry about us," said Lucy.

"Drew! Come on," shouted Michael and he was out the door.

Drew gave Lucy a quick kiss and let her go, running after his brothers."

"I guess we should go, too." Josie gingerly hugged both women.

"Thanks for loaning us your husbands," said Gabe as he hugged the women, too.

Josie and Gabe went out to their horses and mounted. Josie sucked in her breath and then groaned. Together they rode the short way to the barn. In less than fifteen minutes all four of Gabe's brothers rode out to join them.

"Let's go," said Gabe, holding a lantern in one hand and the reins in the other.

They rode the distance as quickly as possible in the full moon light and the lantern light. Still the trip was almost two hours to get to the cabin in the dark.

Gabe killed the lantern and they stopped about thirty yards from the cabin. A light could be seen around the edges of the window and from under the door.

"The darkness is giving us the cover we need. Leave the horses here. We're quieter on our feet. As soon as you can, give us a signal of some kind. Something so we'll know you've reached your destination and we can go forward."

"You'll hear our boyhood birdcall," said Jason.

The six of them split up on the path to the cabin. The brothers walking out toward the beaver pond where they would circle around to the cabin and come in on the backside.

Gabe and Josie waited until they heard a magpie's call before riding into the clearing where they could be seen by Devlin.

Sure enough as they approached the house, a rifle barrel appeared out the window.

"Stay where you are," Devlin shouted from inside the cabin.

Gabe and Josie stopped.

She saw the brothers moving into position. Jason on the side of the window and the other three on the side of the door.

"Did you bring the money?"

Gabe held up the saddle bags but didn't say anything.

"Good. I'm sending Mattie out to get them."

The door opened.

At the same moment, Jason grabbed the rifle and shoved it skyward. The bullet that would have been for either Gabe or Josie missed.

Jason held the rifle while Adam, Drew and Michael entered the cabin.

Gabe and Josie, holding her side, hurried forward.

Mattie, carrying Etta, ran out the door, followed by Walt and Bobby.

Jason pulled the rifle through the window and a moment later, Devlin exited, with his hands raised high, followed by Michael who held his gun on

Devlin. The man stumbled over his own feet but righted himself again. They walked over to Gabe and Josie, who hugged the kids.

Gabe stepped away from the happy reunion.

"You're headed to jail, Devlin. You tried to blackmail us and sell your kids."

Devlin straightened to his full height with was about the same as Josie's five feet, seven inches.

"I didn't do anything wrong. I can sell my kids if I want. You better check with your sheriff."

Gabe ran his hand behind his neck.

Josie looked at him, unable to believe that something so barbaric was legal. "Is he right? Can parents sell their children, legally?"

Gabe gazed at her, the skin between his eyebrows wrinkled. "I don't know. Anything is possible, I suppose. We'll check with the sheriff."

Josie felt bile rise in her throat and held her stomach. "Oh, my God, I think I'm going to be sick. Let's take the kids back to the house and not talk about this in front of them."

"You're right. Of course. Michael, will you escort Devlin to the sheriff's office and ask Brand to hold him until I come in tomorrow to press charges. He can ride Star. We'll take the kids in the wagon."

"Sure will." Michael put Devlin on the horse and then tied his hands to the saddle.

Gabe tied Storm to the back of the wagon and he drove while Josie sat in the back with the kids. Her ribs were killing her, every bump the wagon rolled over felt like a giant hole to her. Once the got the children home and they would settle them in their beds and she would take a seven drop dose of laudanum before she went to bed. She didn't even care, actually didn't want for Gabe to hold her. She just wanted to fall into a pain-free sleep.

Michael took Devlin to the sheriff's office. The rest of them went to Gabe's.

Once they got the children in bed, the brothers, Gabe and Josie sat on the porch and talked.

Josie sat in the swing, her pulse raced and her stomach turned over again and again. "Well, if he won't go to jail for trying to sell his children, then I'll press charges and he can go to jail for beating me up. That's still illegal, isn't it?"

"It is. We'll just have to see what the sheriff says tomorrow. Are you ready for bed?"

"I'm more than ready."

The next morning Mattie cooked breakfast and Gabe took it to Josie in bed.

She was so tired and sore, she could barely sit up in bed. Getting up and getting dressed was beyond her pain threshold.

Gabe sat in the rocking chair he'd pulled up next to the bed.

"How are you this morning?"

"Awful. I hurt so bad I almost wish I was dead."

"I know you're hurting, but I don't want to hear anything like that again."

Mattie came in carrying a cup.

"I brought you a fresh cup of coffee, Josie."

"Thank you. I appreciate it very much."

Gabe stood. "If you ladies will excuse me, I think I'll join the boys in the kitchen."

Mattie watched Gabe leave and then she sat in the rocker and looked down into her lap. She crushed her skirt in her hands. "May I ask you a question?"

Josie sipped the coffee Mattie brought her. "Of course."

"Why?" She cocked her head to one side. "Why did you take us in? You don't take in every kid you find abandoned. Why us?"

"To be honest, I think you remind me of me. Finding you in the circumstances we did made me appreciate the upbringing I had. Even when Mama and I were abandoned, we had each other. I still had a parent. You and your siblings didn't have that and I wanted you to know you are wanted."

Mattie sat and let her tears fall. "When he left I knew he wasn't coming back. I prayed that he really did get killed so I'd never have to see him again. He took all the money and the rifle. He left us the shotgun and the food. You can't kill a deer with a shotgun."

"Not unless you were really close and even then probably not. How did you survive?"

Mattie wiped her cheeks with the palms of her hands. "We fished a lot, but we stayed hungry most of the time. Walt and I did our best to give Bobby and Etta enough food, but that was difficult. Sometimes we'd rob passersby like you, though we usually got away with the theft. Why'd you follow me? You could have just ridden off."

"I saw the size of the foot print and knew that a child had taken our food. We knew that you probably needed the food but also that you might also be in trouble. Gabe and I couldn't just ride away knowing children might need our help."

Mattie stared Josie in the face. "I didn't want to like you. You have Gabe and for that, I didn't want to like you."

Josie smiled. "I know. You're a lot like me, but you don't want to hear that either. Do you still have a crush on Gabe?"

"No. I know that nothing can ever come of those feelings, besides, Luke wants to court me."

She looked down.

Not before Josie saw her cheeks blush pink.

"He seems like a nice young man. I was quite taken with him."

Mattie's head snapped up. "You already got a husband."

Josie laughed and then moaned. "That hurts. I shouldn't laugh. I'm not planning on trading Gabe in any time soon. You've nothing to worry about from me. Margaret is still sick, so you and I...meaning you...need to make a meal and feed yourself and your siblings. I'd help you cook but I think I'm confined to the bed for a few days."

Mattie shook her head. "I can't get over the fact that you're a girl and you don't know how to cook."

The smile left Josie's face. "I never had the time or the need to learn. I was out taking care of the animals, hunting and fishing, chopping wood for the stove and the fireplace. I sold furs in Tacoma, along with elk and deer meat. Would have sold them bear, too, but, thank God, I never ran into one to shoot. Anyway, I never had time to be a girl or learn to cook. Mama did that and she kept the house too."

"Wow. I never knew you did so much. How did you meet Gabe?"

"It's a long story, suffice it to say, we fell in love with you and want to keep you kids together. Is that so bad?"

Mattie shrugged. "No, it's not and we thank you very much, even though we haven't said so."

"You don't have to thank us. Any decent person would have done the same."

The young woman shook her head. "That's not true and you know it. Very few, if any, people would do what you and Gabe did."

Gabe walked in from outside. "What did I do? Am I in trouble, I deny everything."

She and Mattie laughed.

Josie groaned held her side. "Please no more laughing. It's excruciating."

"No." Josie cocked an eyebrow. "You're not in trouble. Should you be? What have you done that you're feeling so guilty?"

Gabe held up his hands. "Nothing. Honest. I was just trying to be funny."

"Very well. Mattie is going to give me another cooking lesson."

"Well, I'll try," said Mattie.

"Speaking of cooking, Josie, you are not doing any. You need to rest for a couple of days and let your ribs heal." said Gabe, "Beside. I wanted to know if either of you has any desire to attend the church social on Sunday. If you want to go, you need to stay in bed until then. Everyone will bring something for the main meal and something for dessert."

"I think the social sounds like fun and I promise to be a good girl," said Josie. She looked at Mattie "Will you cook something we can take?"

"Sure. I'll make a cake and fried chicken. That should do the trick."

"Sounds wonderful," said Gabe.

Mattie stood. "I better see what we have to prepare for lunch. See you later. Rest."

Mattie gave her a quick nod and turned toward the door but Josie saw the tears in her eyes.

Maybe she was making headway with Mattie. At least the girl wasn't openly hostile any longer.

How will she feel when I put her father in jail? Will she care? Or was she speaking the truth when she said she wished he was dead?

CHAPTER 12

The day of the church social arrived. Josie was still fuming that the sheriff had to let Vincent Devlin go. Even his assault of her wasn't enough to keep him in jail for more than a few days.

She closed her eyes and took a deep breath. Nothing would spoil her day. She had a surprise for Gabe. She'd asked Rachel to make a dress for her and the one she made was beautiful. Luckily Rachel took the measurements before Devlin injured Josie. She didn't think she could stand that long now. As for a corset, that was definitely out. She didn't need one to give her an hourglass figure, she had one naturally.

Her dress was bright yellow and complimented Josie's brown hair and eyes. The neckline was lower than Josie would have liked it, but Rachel and Lucy, assured her the style was very fashionable. It had turned out a little shorter than she would have liked, but she noticed a lot of the brides wore their dresses and skirts above the ankle because the streets were so often muddy.

She found the combs which were the last gifts the tinker had given her. They were just plain tortoise-shell, but were very pretty. She used the combs to pull her hair back behind her ears, leaving the length to fall down her back.

They didn't have a mirror other than the small one Gabe used to shave and so she didn't know what the final effect was. When she was finally dressed she went out into the living room and figured her family would tell her how she appeared.

When she entered, Gabe glanced up, smiled, and then went back to his paper. Suddenly he put down the paper and stared at her. This time he looked her up and down slowly.

"You look lovely. I know how you feel about dresses, but I think your appearance is wonderful."

"You do, Josie," said Mattie. "You look great."

Josie smiled, gazed at the floor and swiveled from side to side.

"Good. I was afraid it was too short and people would make fun of me since they could see my boots. I don't have any other shoes."

Mattie shook her head and stood. "See, mine is just as short."

She's a school girl and different fashion rules apply, but I hope my dress will do.

Josie looked around for the boys and Etta. "Okay. Good. Are we all ready to go? Do you have extra clothes and nappies for Etta? She's bound to need them."

Mattie lifted a flour sack. "Got them right here."

Gabe carefully put his arm around Josie and gave her a quick kiss.

"You look beautiful," he whispered in her ear. Then he spoke louder to include Mattie. "Are you ladies ready? I've got the buggy out front ready to go?"

Mattie picked up Etta and Josie took the bag of clothes since it was the lightest and she wanted to help. Walt and Bobby carried the food. Mattie fried three chickens and baked a yellow cake with boiled icing. It was a definite treat for Josie because her mama didn't know how to bake.

They picked up Wilma and then drove to the church. The ride distance wasn't great, only about a mile, but with all they had to carry, the buggy was much appreciated.

As they entered the church, Josie heard an undercurrent within the din of voices. Some of the brides stared at her wide eyed and talked behind their hands.

"Do you see her?"

"She's finally wearing a dress but the garment looks like it was made for a school-girl."

"It's so short and it doesn't fit her. Look how it pulls across her chest."

"And look how she's wearing her hair. Scandalous."

"She's too old to wear her hair down."

With every step, Josie held back the tears, until the comment about her hair. She couldn't take anymore. She shoved the bag of Etta's clothes at Gabe and went up to the women.

"You have no right to judge me. At least I didn't sell myself to find a husband."

The four women reddened and stared at her wide-eyed.

Finally a skinny woman named Letty Linley, stepped forward.

"Forgive me, Josie. You're right we are being catty and that is not well-done of any of us. We have no right to judge you when you actually look quite nice, more so than we do, which is why we are jealous. Please forgive me."

"Me, too," echoed the other three women."

She walked back to Gabe and Matty.

"I was just trying to make you happy. Trying to be the woman you want."

He kissed her hair.

"Josie, love, I don't care what you wear. You're my wife and I'm proud to have you as my wife."

Josie stiffened in his arms. What did he think he was doing throwing around the word 'love' like that? He didn't love her. He couldn't. She didn't believe men didn't fell in love at the drop of a hat...like she had.

173

She pulled back…away from his warm body, his comforting arms and quiet words.

"I'm fine now. We need to make sure the kids are okay. Mattie shouldn't have to watch them all the time." She held up her hand as he started to speak. "I know they took care of themselves for a while, but they were alone in the woods, not out among people who say things and do things that might hurt them."

Gabe stared.

His eyes were sad, no merriment twinkled in them.

"All right if that's what you want. Just remember, I'm here when you want me. I'm not going anywhere."

Josie gave him a curt nod and turned back to the fire. She couldn't bear to see the disappointment on his face.

Josie put her hair in her standard braid, dressed in denims that fit her a little snug and her special white blouse. She looked much the same as she did for her wedding to Gabe. Except for the holster with her Colt in it. She didn't usually wear it, but she felt the need today.

When she was done, she walked back to the church and found Gabe with all the kids except Mattie. She sat across from Gabe and watched Walt and Bobby play with their baby sister. Josie wasn't sure what they were playing, but Etta giggled and ran around after one boy and then the other.

"Where's Mattie?" She grinned. "Did Luke come spirit her away for a quiet rendezvous?"

"No, she needed to take care of her private business. That was quite a while ago though she should have been back by now."

"I'll go see if I can find her."

Josie walked toward the back of the church when she saw him coming toward her...Vincent Devlin. Her eyes widened. The man had the gall to smile at her.

She put her hand on her pistol in the holster at her side. "What are you doing here, Devlin. You're not welcome. This event is for members of the community which you clearly are not."

He stopped but his smile never faded.

"Now, Miz Talbot...Josie...don't get so worked up or you may never see Mattie again."

"What? Where is she you lowlife piece of—"

"Now Josie, before you get carried away, in your heart of hearts you know I have her. You can't see her around here anywhere, can you? I'll tell you where she is when you pay me the five-hundred dollars I've asked for."

Lord I want to kill him. What kind of person does that make me? Unfortunately, I can't. I won't risk Mattie.

"We don't pay ransom."

"Then I guess you'll never see Mattie…alive…again."

Her mouth grew dry and sweat broke out on her back, Devlin would let his own child die rather than give up his chance for a lot of money. And what would keep him from taking one of the other children?

"All right. We'll pay you and then you get out of town and never come back. I swear if I see you in Seattle, I'll shoot you myself."

"When you give me the money, I'll tell you where Mattie is. You've already tried to fool me once."

Josie shook her head and pointed to him. "You have Mattie at the trade in two hours on the west side of Dormitory One. If you don't bring her, no trade will be made and my husband will beat the location out of you. Nothing will stop him, do you understand?"

Josie saw Devlin's Adam's apple bob in his throat.

"Yeah. I understand. She'll be there. You have my word. By the way, don't bring the law. I see the sheriff and I'll see that you never see Mattie alive again."

"You'd kill her? She's your child."

"I don't care. I think we understand each other."

Devlin turned and disappeared back into the crowd of picnickers.

Josie ran to where Gabe and the kids were.

"Gabe!" she shouted as soon as she saw him.

The skin between his brows formed lines and his eyebrows furrowed. "Josie. What's wrong? Where's Mattie?"

"Devlin has her and won't give her up until we pay him. He said he'd kill her if we brought the sheriff. I told him we wouldn't. Gabe I don't want to take a chance with her life. We don't know where she is, unlike last time. I told him he'd better bring her with him or you'd beat the location out of him. Did I do wrong?"

He wrapped his arms around her, careful of her ribs.

"No. You didn't do wrong. You're right we can't take a chance with Mattie's life. Let's gather the kids and take them with us to Jason's. I can't think of anywhere safer. Plus we need to get the money from him. I don't have five hundred dollars available, but he will for the business."

"Oh, Gabe..." Eyes that held only determination, just as she felt.

"We're not letting him get away with this extortion. He shouldn't be rewarded for selling his children."

"He won't. We'll have the saddlebags and some of the money, so the appearance will be that they are full of the ransom, but they won't be. Hopefully, he won't find out that fact until we have Mattie safe and sound."

She nodded. "Sounds like a plan and if he tries to keep Mattie or to hurt her, I'll kill him Gabe. I owe him for my ribs. I'm just giving you fair warning."

Gabe raised an eyebrow and took her hands in his. "I won't let you commit murder. We'll take him to the sheriff."

They gathered the kids and Wilma, put them in the buggy and drove straight to Jason's home.

Josie handed Etta to Walt and then she got out of the buggy and took Etta back. They followed Gabe into the house without knocking.

"Jason!" Gabe shouted.

"Stop bellowing, little brother. What's the matter?"

"Devlin took Mattie and is holding her for five-hundred dollars ransom. He's got her someplace where we won't find her. We agreed to pay but he has to have Mattie with him."

The skin between Jason's eyebrows creased and his eyebrows went down. "I don't have that kind of money on hand, you know that."

Gabe shook his head. "I intend to fool him. But I need a hundred dollars to make it look real and we need paper, newspaper, anything we can cut to simulate the rest of the money. Hopefully, by the time he figures the ruse out we'll be far away."

Jason ran his hand behind his neck. Josie had noticed he often did this when he didn't like the answer he was given. Gabe ran his hand through his hair instead.

"All right. When do you have to meet him?" Jason looked intently at Gabe.

Josie answered. "In about an hour and forty-five minutes by Dormitory One."

"I guess we'd better get busy then, shouldn't we?" said Jason.

"We better if we expect to have the saddlebag ready with phony money." *What if he figures out the ruse before Mattie gets away?*

CHAPTER 13

Gabe and Josie took the saddle-bags of phony money and rode in the buggy down to the dormitory. When they arrived, Devlin was waiting...a gun in one hand and grasping Mattie's arm with the other.

Josie took the saddle-bags from Gabe and walked over to Devlin.

"Here's your blood money." Josie threw the bags at Devlin's feet.

He pushed Mattie toward Josie. The girl stumbled, but righted herself quickly and ran to Josie.

She gathered Mattie into her arms and gave her back to Devlin. If anyone was getting shot today it would be Josie, not Mattie.

The two of them had only taken a few steps when Devlin let out a scream of rage.

"Run, Mattie, run."

Josie drew her pistol and fired at Devlin, intending just to scare him, not kill him. She stood her ground giving Mattie as much cover as she could. Gabe was also shooting at Devlin.

Devlin's shots weren't so kind. She heard the zing of a bullet past her head. He was definitely trying to kill her. She was lucky he wasn't a better shot.

She finally turned and followed Mattie, running as fast as she could.

Gabe gave her cover and continued firing at Devlin, to keep him off kilter so he didn't shoot Josie.

Josie felt something like fire in her left side and she stumbled, falling to the ground. She got up and holding her side she ran as fast as she could. When she looked back, Gabe was still firing at Devlin, but his aim improved considerably. He shot the man in the stomach and in the knee which made him drop, clutching his stomach in pain.

Josie reached Gabe just as Devlin took his gun and aimed at her.

Gabe fired just as Devlin did.

Devlin's shot missed.

Gabe's didn't.

Vincent Devlin wouldn't be giving anyone any trouble ever again.

Gabe swept Josie into his arms and ran as fast as he could into the dormitory.

"Karen! Karen Martell," he called out at the top of his lungs.

Mattie followed him inside.

The brides in the dormitory were gathered in front of the windows and had watched the gunfight.

Karen came out of her room, her children, Larry and Patty, peeking out the door. "I'm here, Gabe. I was keeping the children away from the windows. What is—oh my. I really wish you Talbots would stop getting shot. I really don't want gunshot wounds to be my specialty."

"Please take care of her."

"Certainly. Follow me."

Gabe followed Karen to the kitchen, with Mattie after him.

"Josie, can you sit up? It looks like the bullet hit you in the side," said Karen.

"Sure. I think I can."

"Good. Gabe, set her over here on the counter by the sink," Karen instructed. To Mattie she said, "Sit at the table please, or you can go to my room and play with my children."

Her chin went up. "I'll stay if Josie doesn't mind."

Josie nodded. "Fine by me."

Gabe followed Karen's instructions.

"Okay, take off your shirt, please," said Karen. She set her doctor's bag on the counter next to Josie.

Josie did as she was told. She didn't even worry if anyone watched since she hurt too much to care.

Gabe helped her take off her shirt and then roll up her chemise. Now Karen had unfettered access to the wound.

"The bullet went clean through and the bright red blood tells me it didn't hit any organs. I'll clean the wounds, stitch them and then wrap your ribs. You'll be very sore for some time, but I'll take out the stitches in about ten days."

"Thanks, Karen. I appreciate you being here," said Gabe.

Josie nodded. "And I'm very happy you're here. I can't imagine having this big lug sew me up, but you know, even so I'm not feeling very well." She suddenly felt sick to her stomach and so dizzy.

She passed out into Gabe's arms.

"Josie. Karen what's the matter with her?"

Mattie leapt from her chair. "Josie!"

She lay quietly as he held her.

Karen looked at Mattie. "She's okay, Mattie." Then she gazed up at Gabe. "Let her be until I finish stitching her side, then I'll wake her up."

Gabe nodded. "Whatever you say, Doc." He stared down at his wife. Josie. His wife, who he cared more about than he was willing to admit to her. Did he love her?

Karen tied off the last stitch and then dug around in her doctor bag and came out with a small bottle.

She opened the bottle and waved it under Josie's nose.

Josie gasped and opened her eyes. She waved her arm almost hitting Karen's hand holding the smelling salts, and then groaned in pain.

"What happened? Where am I?"

Gabe held on to her, making her feel safe. "You were shot, sweetheart. Now you're in Dormitory One, sitting on the kitchen counter with my arms wrapped around you."

"I remember now." She closed her eyes tight and grimaced as a wave of pain washed over her. "You had to kill Vincent Devlin. He left you no choice."

"That's right. And he shot you before he died."

"That's why I hurt. Great Scot."

"Yeah," said Gabe. "Karen cleaned and sewed the wound closed and now I'm taking you home and putting you in bed."

"I think that sounds like a good idea."

Gabe chuckled. "I thought you might."

Karen helped her dress since she couldn't lift her arm without it hurting.

"I'm not tucking your shirt in your pants. I'll just have to take it out again when we get home," said Gabe.

Josie nodded. "That's fine."

"Gabe, do you still have laudanum at home?" asked Karen.

"Yeah. I'll give her some before putting her to bed."

"Five drops ought to do it, in a half glass of water."

"Got it."

Gabe looked at Josie.

"Can you walk, sweetheart?"

Josie nodded and cocked an eyebrow. "Do I look like I'm crippled?"

"No, but you've been through a traumatic experience and I thought—"

"I'm fine. Let's get home to the kids. Where's Mattie?"

"I'm here," said the girl from her seat at the table. "I'll be right behind you."

Josie stood and took a step before collapsing into Gabe's waiting arms.

She couldn't believe how weak she was. Good grief, she was shot in the side not the legs, but her legs were wobbly and wouldn't hold her weight.

Gabe shook his head. "Okay. That's enough." He scooped her up, walked out to the buggy and set her on the front seat. "Nothing is wrong with needing help now and again."

She sighed. "That's true. Until you came along I learned to only rely on myself. Being abandoned for whatever reason will do that to a person." She looked down at Mattie. "Isn't that true, Mattie?"

The girl stood waiting for Gabe to help her up into the back seat of the surrey.

When he came around to her, she took his hand and stepped up into the buggy.

"That's right. Walt and I relied on each other. No one else, until now."

Gabe walked around to his side. "Agreed but now you have me. We need to learn to rely on each other."

She inclined her head just a bit. "I suppose you're right."

"Of course, I am."

When they reached the house, Gabe set the brake and then came around and helped first Mattie and then Josie to the ground. He started to pick her up again.

Instead, she put her hand on his arm and shook her head.

"I don't want to scare the kids. Let me walk in holding your arm."

"All right." He held out his arm.

She slipped her hand through the crook in his elbow and leaned into him.

"I think I'm hurt worse than I thought."

He patted her hand where it rested in the bend of his arm. "You've been shot. Did you expect to just go right back as though nothing happened?"

Her legs were shaky as she walked and her stride was very short and slow. "I honestly don't know what I thought. I've never been shot before. I'm worried about the kids. How will they feel knowing their father is dead?"

Mattie walked behind them. "He's been dead to us for months. The fact the state is real this time won't make any difference. He abandoned us long ago."

Josie stopped and turned to Mattie. "Regardless of the terrible parent he was, he was still your father and I'm sorry he was the way he was. You, all of you, deserved so much more."

Mattie nodded and then without warning, she wrapped her arms around Josie and wept.

Josie, unmindful of her injury, returned the hug and let the girl cry. She'd been through so much in her young life. Josie had, too.

Josie knew if there was any way for her to help Mattie take the right path, she would.

They walked into the house, Josie with her arm around Mattie's shoulders and Gabe following behind with a smile on his face.

Josie wondered what made him smile. Was he glad Mattie and Josie were getting along?

Seven days later

Josie was so sick of being in bed she thought she would go stir crazy. Deciding this was nuts, she'd been in bed for a week, she got up, dressed even though her side definitely hurt when she raised her arm to put on her chemise. She ignored the pain and finished dressing. She would have breakfast with her family whether Gabe liked it or not.

When she walked into the kitchen, Gabe stood and frowned.

"What are you doing up? Karen said ten days in bed. Only seven have passed."

"Seven is as many as you get. If, okay *when*, I get tired I'll go back to bed for a nap, but I have things to do."

"Nothing that Walt and I can't get done between us. If you insist on being out of bed, then you need to spend your time on the sofa, reading or knitting or something."

Walt, upon hearing his name, looked up, then at each of them and took his leave.

He apparently wanted no part of his new parent's argument. "I don't know how to knit and I'm tired of reading. I think I've read every book in the house."

"Then I'll bring you new ones from Jason's."

She went over to Gabe and wrapped her arms loose around his waist. Just that was enough to make her groan but she didn't give in to the pain. "Why don't I just take the buggy and go to Jason and Rachel's myself? I can visit with Rachel and Lucy for a while. Anything to get out of this house."

Gabe was quiet for a moment then furrowed his brows before speaking.

"You would just visit and pick out some new books. Is that correct?"

"Yes. Nothing strenuous." She raised her hand and made a cross over her heart. "I promise. Cross my heart. Mattie can come with me if she would like."

"Well, I suppose it won't hurt for you to visit."

She hugged him, keeping her arms around his waist so she didn't have to lift them around his neck.

"Thank you. I'll go tell Mattie."

"You do that."

She turned and left the barn, but saw that Gabe had a smile on his face.

Glad as she was that he was happy, she wasn't ready to tell him what she suspected…that she was pregnant. It wasn't out of the question. They'd been married for almost two months now. But what if he runs? What if he abandons her like her father and Elias did? She knew now that both her father died and Elias had been killed and hadn't really abandoned her, but that didn't stop the feelings she'd had for all these years. The facts didn't take away the yearning, the fear of getting close to a man. All those feelings remained, though she tried to not equate them with Gabe who had never been anything but kind.

Though the fact that they didn't love each other, actually that he didn't love her, wouldn't go away from her mind or her heart. And what if she was wrong?

No, it was better not to say anything…yet.

CHAPTER 14

Saturday, November 11, 1865

Josie and Gabe had spent the last couple of weeks
attending to the kids. Making sure to be available
for them. Walt and Gabe took Bobby fishing. Josie
was slowly learning to cook, since Margaret ended
up getting married after she recovered from her
illness.

Thankfully, Mattie was a patient teacher and
more than once had saved dinner from being
ruined.

Last week they had all traveled to Olympia
where Gabe and Josie filed the paperwork
necessary to adopt the kids legally.

Now she stood in the mercantile looking at
dress material. She was starting to show, and she
thought hiding in a dress easier than in her regular

clothes. With her fancy sewing machine, Rachel could make her a dress in a couple of days and this time Josie would make sure to show up at all fittings. That fiasco at the church social had been her fault. She'd been too busy for fittings, always finding something else to do when she was supposed to go get measured and go for the fittings. She had told Rachel to do the best she could. Josie didn't think it had been necessary but she discovered she was wrong.

A couple entered the store and they were definitely from out of town. Josie didn't recognize them and they had accents like many of the brides did.

The woman was average height and wore a gray walking suit with hoops that were about three feet from her on any side. Josie hadn't see clothes like that since she was last in Olympia.

The man wore a suit with a long top coat open in deference to the warm November weather. They walked to the counter where Fred Longmire stocked the brightly colored penny candy. The same candy the tinker had brought her almost every time he came and that she would purchase to take home for the kids when she bought her material.

"We're George and Doris Eggleston and we're looking for Mattie Devlin. Do you know where we might find her?"

"Sure do but you might want to talk to her soon-to-be mother over there." He pointed to where Josie stood in front of the bolts of cloth. "Josie," Fred shouted. "These folks are looking for Mattie."

Josie's gut clenched. She didn't like that strangers were looking for Mattie. She picked up a bolt of yellow calico and walked to the counter.

"May I help you?"

"Yes, ma'am. I'm Doris and this is my husband George Eggleston. We're Mattie's aunt and uncle. Her mother, Millie, was my youngest sister."

Josie's hands began to sweat when she noticed Doris had the same red hair as Mattie. She wiped her hand on her pants and held it out to Doris who daintily shook her hand and then to George who had a good grip and shook hands well.

"What are you doing here?" asked Josie, her stomach in knots.

"We came to see if we could help Vincent with the children since my sister's death."

"I see."

"I'm afraid it took us much longer than we anticipated to get here but I'm sure Vincent would have understood."

Josie tilted her head and cocked an eyebrow. "Did he know you were coming?"

"Yes," said George. "But we were supposed to be here almost a year ago. We sent a letter and told him we were coming later than expected. We had trouble selling the house and had to wait for the sale to close."

Josie's mouth was dry and she started to shake. "So you're planning on moving here?"

"Yes, we thought it would be less traumatic for the children to remain where they are comfortable."

"You want the kids to live with you I take it." Josie stomach clenched like she's just been hit in the gut.

"Yes, of course," said Doris. "We weren't blessed with any children of our own and having them will fulfill my lifelong dream. I understand that Vincent is dead. We were told that as soon as we asked someone for him."

"Yes, what happened was quite the scandal. You see he tried to sell his children."

The woman raised her hand to her mouth. "Oh, no. He couldn't have. He was such a doting father to Mattie and Walt."

Josie tried to keep the anger she still felt from her voice. "Apparently things changed."

Doris leaned into her husband.

"Oh, George. What are we to do now?"

"No choice. We'll buy them back."

"You would do that for me?"

He held her hand and the look on his face made Josie want to cry. She'd never seen love before, not like this, between a man and a woman. The look was pure, simple, unadulterated love. Unmistakable. A look she'd never seen on Gabe's face, much less when he looked at her.

"You'll buy them back? How is this offer any better than selling them? If you'll come with me

I'll take you to the children. Buying them back is not necessary. I'm Josie Talbot, by the way. My husband and I were preparing to adopt the children and my husband killed Vincent Devlin."

The short walk to Josie's home was quiet. She didn't know what to say to them. *Why don't you go back to where you came from,* didn't seem to be appropriate.

When they arrived at the house, Josie showed them into the living room.

"Please, have a seat. I'll get Mattie. She's usually in the kitchen. She does all of our cooking since Margaret, our housekeeper, was ill and then got married. Forgive me. I ramble when I'm nervous."

"It's all right, my dear," said Doris. "I understand how you must feel. You're forced to be nice when we are going to try and take the children."

Josie nodded. "Yes. I'm glad you understand. Gabe and I have come to love the children very much. They are the reason we married so quickly. If you'll wait here, I'll get Mattie."

Josie went into the kitchen and found Mattie feeding oatmeal to Etta. Well, actually she let the baby feed herself and she wore more oatmeal than she ate.

When Etta saw Josie, she grinned.

"Mama."

Josie's heart melted. Etta had never called her Mama before. She couldn't help the tears that welled in her eyes.

"Mattie, some people here to see you."

"Oh, who are they?"

"You'll see. Go on now. I'll clean up Etta and be in right behind you."

Mattie left and Josie wiped Etta from head to toe with a wet washcloth. When she was presentable, Josie took her to join the rest of her family. The boys were out with Gabe in the barn mucking stalls and caring for the horses.

When she entered the living room with Etta, Mattie sat in the chair across from her aunt and uncle who occupied the sofa.

Josie saw that Mattie was not happy about seeing her aunt and uncle. Josie knew the feeling well. "How long has it been since you saw one another?"

"Too long," said Doris.

"Not long enough," said Mattie who sat with her arms crossed over her chest.

"Mattie," said Josie, gently, surprised at the vehemence in the girls voice. "Your aunt and uncle came a long way to be with you and your siblings. You should be happy they cared for you so much."

The girl relaxed a bit.

"I'm sorry. It's just that we were getting to where we were settled and we like it here. Gabe and Josie love us." She looked over at Josie, her eyes wide and her eyebrows scrunched. "Don't you?"

Josie sat on the arm of the chair Mattie sat in and held Etta, who sucked her thumb and leaned on Josie's chest. "Of course, we do. Very much."

"Then why can't we stay with you?"

"Because you have family here who want you as much as we do." Josie looked over at the Egglestons. "I hope you'll be settling here in Seattle. We'd like for the children to be close, and Mattie has a young man who has started calling on her."

"Yes, we had planned on staying here. George sold his business and we sold the house, so our income is not reliant on having to work, although George might open an office here. Isn't Mattie a little young to have a young man?"

"She is fourteen, we hope they will court for some time before marriage. Mattie is aware of our wishes. What do you do, Mr. Eggleston?"

"I'm an attorney."

"Oh, a lawyer. Well, I can't say the residents of Seattle would keep you busy, but we have need of a lawyer here, if for no other reason than we wouldn't have to go all the way to Olympia every time we need your advice."

He nodded. "Well, that's something I'll consider."

"Is the baby Etta?" asked Doris, dipping her head toward Josie.

"Yes," said Josie. "Would you like to hold her? She'll probably want to play with that beautiful brooch you're wearing."

"Well," Doris jerked backwards. "We can't have that. It's got a sharp pin holding it on. She could hurt herself."

Mattie looked at her aunt and her shoulders relaxed a bit.

As much as Josie didn't want to admit it, the kids would probably be better off with family than with her and Gabe. But without the kids, what held her and Gabe together?

She rested her hand on her stomach. She thought about the baby they had made. It was a blessing, but not one she would use to trap Gabe in a loveless marriage. He had a right to find love. She already had, she just didn't know if he loved her back. Neither of them had used the words, said them to each other. Was he just afraid, like she was?

"Have you checked into the Seattle Inn?" asked Josie.

"Yes, we did," said George. He sat back and crossed his legs. "We did that first thing. We didn't want to be carrying our luggage with us or have the trunks sitting out on the dock."

"Good. You'll have to come, or just stay, for supper. Mattie is a fine cook."

Mattie smiled and sat up straighter.

Quiet reined in the room. Suddenly the door opened and Gabe and the boys entered.

197

"Well, Looks like we've got company," said Gabe.

Josie stood and walked over and took him by the arm.

"Gabe, these folks are George and Doris Eggleston. They are the kids' aunt and uncle."

She stepped behind Walt and Bobby and held them still while George and Doris greeted them. First they shook hands with Gabe, then Walt and Bobby.

"We're so pleased to see you children. We haven't seen you since Bobby was a baby. What is that six years ago?"

"You know how old I am?" asked Bobby with a big smile.

"Yes." Doris leaned down to be more on his level. "Your mommy was my youngest sister. I loved her very much."

Walt sat on the arm of Mattie's chair. Josie noticed his arm was around Mattie's shoulder, as if they were a united front. Bobby stood on the other side of the chair.

"Why didn't you come before? Mama's been dead a long time."

"We couldn't," said George. "I wrote your father and told him we would be later than anticipated. He must not have shared that information with you."

"He didn't share anything with us except his desire to be rid of us," said Mattie.

"I'm so sorry about that." Doris' frowned, her mouth downturned and her eyes narrowed. "If we had known how he felt, I would have come by myself and taken care of you."

"We took care of ourselves until Josie and Gabe found us. Now they want us to be their kids and you expect us to just say no and come live with you?"

Mattie's words were punctuated by suppressed rage. Her body stiffened and her hands formed fists.

Josie thought it best to end this interview. "Doris, George, why don't you two come back for supper around six. We have a lot to discuss with the kids and they with us."

The Eggleston's stood. Josie took Etta from Doris who put the pin in her pocket so she could hold the baby.

"Mama," said Etta when Josie picked her up. "Mama like baby?"

Josie nearly cried. "Oh, yes sweetheart. Josie loves the baby. Josie loves Etta." She looked around at Mattie, Walt and Bobby. "Josie loves your brothers and sister, too." She kissed the baby's cheek.

If the Eggleston's didn't know how difficult this was before, perhaps now they knew.

Gabe moved next to Josie and put his arm around her, enveloping her and the baby with his warmth. His strength.

Doris and George left and the kids started talking at once.

"Hold on a minute. One at a time," said Gabe, with a downward motion of his arms. "Let's sit and talk about this."

"What is there to talk about?" Mattie stood with her hands on her hips. "You want us don't you?"

"Of course, we do," said Josie.

Gabe nodded.

"Then we'll stay with you."

"It's not that easy," said Gabe.

"Now that you have family here, we'll have to get their approval for the adoption to go through and I don't know if they will agree." Josie looked at each of the three children individually, finding speaking difficult over the lump in her throat. "You see they want you. They were never blessed with children and helping to raise you four will fulfill a life-long dream of theirs. Of course, Mattie is nearly grown and she has a sweetheart now, so she probably won't be with them for long anyway."

Mattie turned red and looked down.

But not before Josie saw a smile on her lips.

"But Bobby and Etta, especially will be living with them for a long time. And your aunt and uncle want that. They are staying in Seattle so it's not as if we won't see each other all the time. And you know you're always welcome here."

"You sound like you're giving up on us." Walt's shoulders slumped.

"Not at all," said Gabe. He held Josie and Etta close. "We're trying to do what is in everyone's best interest. Your aunt and uncle want you very much. They sold everything and traveled here so they could be with you. How many people do you figure would do that?" He spread his hands in front of him, palms up. Not many I can tell you."

"I want you to talk among yourselves and decide what you want to do. Gabe and I will be in the kitchen when you come to a decision."

Josie took Gabe's hand and led him into the kitchen.

"We have to think about what we're doing if they decide to live with George and Doris. Are we staying married? I'm not sure I want to stay in a marriage without love. I deserve to have someone who loves me and you need to be able to find the person you love, too."

Gabe ran a hand behind his neck. His eyebrows went up and his eyes widened.

"You always do that when you're nervous. So does Jason."

"What?"

"Run your hand behind your neck. Must be a family trait.

He'll tell me he can't love me. I don't think he knows how to say the words.

He looked down at his hand and put it purposefully by his side. "You're right. You deserve someone who is not afraid to love you. I'm not that person. I can't love you or anyone. But if I could, that woman would be you."

She nodded, knowing his response before he said it.

"That's what I thought."

"I'm sorry, Josie."

"Don't be. We knew this could happen going into this marriage."

"Still parting and divorce is not the outcome either of us wished for."

"What did you wish for Gabe?"

Walt came into the kitchen.

"We've made up our minds. You can come back now."

They followed Walt into the living room where he joined Bobby and Etta on the sofa.

Mattie stood with the sofa to her side and did the speaking for the children.

"We've decided to live with Aunt Doris and Uncle George. You're right about them. They didn't have to come out here, but they did. They changed their entire way of life for us, just as you two did. But they are family and we doubt they would give you the permission you need to adopt us either."

"That's fine," said Josie, her mouth so dry she could hardly speak, though her heart was breaking. She knew living with Doris and George was the best thing for the kids, but wished the decision didn't mean the end for her and Gabe."

CHAPTER 15

The day after the kids moved in with George and Doris, Gabe and Josie separated. The house was so quiet with her and the kids gone. It was as empty as his life. She moved back to her mother's home. Almost one week to the day after they parted, Gabe received a telegram from Edward Harrison, his old boss in Massachusetts.

Gabe Talbot. I have a proposition for you. Am dying. You marry Clarissa and the business is yours. Stop. Ed.

Gabe looked again at the telegram. He sat at the kitchen table and read the missive again. He'd always liked Ed Harrison and his business, building whaling ships, was booming. Ten years ago, Clarissa was a mere girl and he had no doubt changed a lot since then. Still, he was surprised that after the Marian fiasco, Ed would still want him as a son-in-law, but Gabe wasn't looking for a love match. Those didn't exist, at least not for him. He refused to even consider being in love. Not after Marian.

He went to the telegraph office and sent an immediate response.

To: Ed Harrison. Will take your offer. Will be there in approximately three to four months. Gabe

Gabe went down to talk to Josie. The house that Josie and her mother lived in was just a few blocks from the center of Seattle. His house, was about half a mile beyond the little enclave of houses that Josie and Wilma moved into. His long legs ate up the distance to Josie's in about five minutes.

He knocked on her mother's door.

Wilma answered.

"What do you want, Gabe?"

"I need to talk to Josie."

Wilma narrowed her eyes. "I don't know that she wants to see you."

"She won't have to see me much longer. I'm leaving Seattle."

She lifted her chin and shook her head. "Why am I not surprised?"

"What's that supposed to mean?"

"Nothing. I'll see if Josie wants to see you."

She didn't invite him in, which in itself seemed

odd, but her attitude about him and Josie divorcing seemed strange, as well.

Josie came to the door.

She looked like hell. Her eyes were red and puffy, her nose looked raw. Her hair hung lankly from her scalp. "Are you sick? You look terrible."

She sighed and tilted her head to one side. "Yes, I'm sick. What do you want? I want to go back to bed."

Gabe let out a long breath. "I just stopped by to tell you I'm leaving. I'm going back to Massachusetts. My old employer presented me with a proposition that given our circumstances I don't feel I can turn down."

"So what, are you filing the divorce papers before you go? I'm sure George would be able to help you with that."

"I'll go see him before I leave. I wanted to see you first. Then I'll say goodbye to the kids."

"Well now you've seen me. I'm going back to bed."

"Goodbye, Josie. I'm sorry our marriage didn't work out."

"So am I, Gabe. More than you'll ever know."

He leaned forward to give her a goodbye kiss.

But she put up her hand and stepped back.

"No reason for us to kiss anymore. Have a happy life."

She turned away and shut the door.

Gabe thought something amiss, but he couldn't put his finger on the difference in her attitude, but something was definitely wrong.

Josie leaned back against the door, silent tears rolling down her face.

Her mother came up to her.

"Oh, honey. I'm so sorry. Are you sure you don't want to tell him about the baby?"

Josie blew out a breath and wiped her face with the palms of her hands.

"I'm sure. I won't use a baby to keep him here."

Wilma frowned. "But you were staying together for the other kids, why not your own child?"

"It's different. Gabe sees an out and he's taking it. He admitted he can't give me what I want or need which is someone to love me, unconditionally."

"All right, I won't interfere, but I think you are making a huge mistake."

"If he realizes how much of a mistake he's making he'll be back and he'll be ready to love me. I have to let him go. Don't you see? If he comes back then he really is mine…forever."

Wilma hugged Josie. They stood, mother and daughter together, holding one another, while Josie cried.

When she finally pulled back from her mother she realized Gabe's leaving was for the best. He would live back east and maybe he'd find a girl he could love.

Josie kissed her mother on the cheek and went back to her bedroom, tears forming again as she walked, her legs feeling almost too heavy to move. She would never get over Gabe. He was her one true love, and she wouldn't look for another.

March 6, 1866

Gabe smiled and shook hands with clients and friends of Ed's, though inside he was cold. His heart wasn't in this. The party was to announce his engagement to Clarissa.

He'd only been here about two weeks but Ed was determined to see his daughter married before he left this earthly realm.

Gabe looked down at Clarissa. Her light blonde hair pulled up into a mass of curls atop her head. Her expression was the same as he felt. She stood next to him a phony smile pasted on her face. She nodded and said all the right things, but the smiles never reached her eyes.

Thomas Evans came over to them. He was Ed's attorney and as he approached, Clarissa perked up. She stood straighter and her smile was real.

"Gabe." Thomas held out his hand. "Congratulations on your engagement."

He next held out his hand to Clarissa. When she put her hand in his, he brought it to his lips and kissed it.

"Goodbye, my dear."

"Thomas, I…" She choked on a sob.

Gabe heard the yearning in Clarissa's tone and realized Thomas is who she loves and she's heartbroken to give him up. Seeing her like this helped him realize the person he needed wasn't here. Wasn't Clarissa any more than he was who she needed and loved.

"Clarissa."

She turned toward him, her big blue eyes shimmering with unshed tears.

"Yes, Gabe."

"I hope you won't hate me, but I can't marry you. I realize that my heart lies in Seattle and always will. May you and Thomas have a wonderful life."

Suddenly, her gaze brightened and she smiled. "Oh, Gabe, thank you. You're a kind man. If I couldn't marry Thomas, I would wish to marry you."

"Thanks. You're a nice woman." Relieved that he wasn't going through with the wedding without knowing his true feelings. He looked over at Thomas and held out his hand. "You're a very lucky man."

Thomas shook Gabe's hand and smiled at Clarissa. "I know."

"Now if you'll excuse me, I have to talk to your father, then pack and see about the next ship out of here."

June 6, 1866
Seattle, Washington Territory

Josie wore the purple dress Rachel gave her from when she'd been pregnant. Josie was a little shorter than Rachel, but it fit well enough. She was as big as a house and hoped the baby would be coming today or tomorrow. Her back hurt and she could hardly walk.

A knock sounded on the front door. Wilma was out, so Josie waddled to the door.

"Yes, what can I help you with?" she asked as she opened the door.

"Josie?"

On the other side of the door was Gabe Talbot.

Josie gasped. "Gabe! What are you doing here? You're supposed to be in Massachusetts married to Clarissa."

"That's not important." Wide-eyed, he pointed at her belly. "You're pregnant. That is important. Why didn't you tell me?"

Josie gripped the door tighter and began to cry.

"I didn't want the reason you stayed to be just the baby. What are you doing here?"

"I came back for you. I couldn't think of anything but you while I was in Massachusetts. Finally when the engagement party was happening, I realized everything, everyone I want and love, is in Seattle. I hopped the first ship sailing this direction and here I am."

Josie placed her hand on the small of her back.

"I guess you might as well come in. Mama's not here, and I think I'm having this baby today."

He lifted an eyebrow and tilted his head. "What makes you think that?"

"Because my water just broke and I need you to go get Karen." She looked down at the puddle near her shoes.

"Holy crap! Forgive my language. Let me help you to bed first."

She didn't feel like arguing. All she wanted was to have this baby. She'd already prepared the bed for the birthing. The oil cloth was down with only a sheet covering it and another sheet to cover her.

Josie took off her robe and hung it over the screen she'd put in the corner of the room to hide the chamber pot.

Gabe helped her into the bed. When she was settled he leaned down and kissed her full on the lips.

"What was that for?" She couldn't decide if she was thrilled he came back for her or still mad that he left.

"Because I've been a fool, Josie." He tucked an errant strand of hair behind her ear. "But I'm not a fool anymore. I'll go get Karen now. Be right back."

He left.

Josie had to wonder if what she'd just experienced was real. She'd dreamed and hoped for him to come back for so long, she couldn't quite believe he was actually here.

She ran her hand over her belly and smiled.

"Your papa is here, little one. You'll get to meet him, after all."

Another pain hit and she cringed, holding her hand on her stomach.

"I know you're anxious now, but I think he's planning on staying this time."

When the pain subsided, Josie rubbed her belly and sang a little tune her mother had sung when she was little. She found the act soothing and apparently so did her child, for he settled down for a bit.

"Josie," Gabe called from the living room. "We're back. Karen's here."

Karen walked into the bedroom followed by an anxious Gabe. He was pale and Josie thought he was probably afraid, remembering how his sister-in-law, Cassie, had died in childbirth.

"Gabe." She patted the bed beside her. "Come lie with me."

He shook his head. "But, the baby—"

"Won't be here for a bit," said Josie. "Karen's got things to do to prepare for our child." She took his hand and placed it on her stomach where the baby was busy moving.

He gazed up at her, eyes wide. "Our baby."

"Yes. Our baby." She finally shared the news she'd wanted to for so long.

"I don't want you to die, Josie. I've only just realized that I love you and I don't want to live without you."

Her eyes filled with tears of joy. She'd waited so long to hear those words.

"I'm not about to die, my love, not now that you're back to stay." She frowned. "You are recommitting to our relationship, aren't you?"

"Oh, yes. I won't be going anywhere...well that's not entirely true. I have one errand to run right away. Try to wait to have the baby until I get back."

"Don't worry," said Karen. "I'll examine her to make sure, but in all likelihood the baby won't be here for a while. In my experience, first babies tend to take their time being born."

Gabe kissed Josie on the forehead, looked into her eyes with something she thought might be longing, and then he left.

Josie groaned with pain.

"Karen, am I really not having this baby for a long while?"

"Now, I didn't say a *long* while. Let me check you, and then I'll let you know for sure. Raise your knees and spread your legs, please."

Josie did exactly as Karen asked.

"Well, well." Karen's eyebrows raised and her eyes widened. "You're having this baby sooner than anticipated. He's already beginning to crown."

Josie looked toward the door. "I hope Gabe gets back from his errand before the baby comes."

A few minutes later, Gabe returned with Reverend Peabody and his wife.

Wilma came into the room as well and grinned at Josie.

Gabe sat on the edge of the bed next to her and took her hand.

"Josie Talbot, would you do me the great honor of becoming my wife, to have and to hold forever? I promise never to let you go and to love you always. What do you say, sweetheart? Marry me again?"

She was quiet a minute, a pain bearing down upon her and she breathed hard until it passed.

"I'll marry you, but you'd better be quick, because I'd really like for this to be done before he gets here."

Gabe smiled. "Yes, ma'am." He looked over at the reverend. "Are you ready, sir."

The man shook his head and smiled back. "This wedding is most unusual, but here goes. Dearly beloved, we are gathered here to join this man and this woman in holy matrimony—"

"Ahhh," moaned Josie and gripped Gabe's hand. "You'd better make this one the short ceremony, Reverend."

He nodded. "Do you Gabriel Talbot, take this woman to be your wedded wife, to have and to hold, from this day forward for as long as you both shall live?

"I do." Gabe looked down at her.

He smiled the sweetest smile Josie had ever seen.

"Do you Josie Talbot, take this man to be your wedded husband, to have and to hold from this day forward until death do you part?"

"I..." She looked up at Gabe. He was so vulnerable now. His heart was on his sleeve and she was the one who could destroy it. But she would care for his heart like it was her own. He was answering all her prayers. "I do."

Gabe physically relaxed with her utterance of those two little words.

She said them just before another contraction made her forget everything except the pain. Her hands pressed hard on her thighs and rubbed them up and down.

"I now pronounce you man and wife. You may kiss the bride," said the reverend as he finished the service.

Gabe bent over and kissed her lips and her forehead.

"Okay, gentlemen, now it's time for you to leave," said Karen.

"I love you, Josie." He squeezed her hand and held it as he stood.

She squeezed it back unable to speak because if she opened her mouth she'd scream. The pain of the birth was almost unbearable and she wanted to shout so badly.

"Out! Now!" said Karen.

As Gabe, the reverend and Mrs. Peabody left, Rachel and Lucy came into the bedroom.

"We're here to help, Karen. What do you need?" said Raychel.

"How did you know to come?" asked Karen.

"Gabe sent Leroy Bates, Billy's friend, to tell us," said Lucy. "And, of course, we dropped everything to come."

"I probably only need one of you to help me but Wilma, I want you to help Josie. You can hold her hand and talk her through the pains."

"Of course." Wilma sat on the bed next to Josie. "I'm here Ladybug. You just squeeze my hand when you're having a contraction. I'll help you through this."

"Thank you, Mama. He came back. He came back for me."

Wilma smiled. "Yes, he did. Just like you said he would."

Josie squeezed her mother's hand as hard as she could and when that wasn't enough, Josie finally screamed with the pain.

Gabe's brothers, Jason and Drew, arrived with their wives and now kept him company in the living room.

"Glad you finally came around," said Drew as he cuffed Gabe's arm. "Seriously, I'm sorry you had to go away to know what we already did...that you loved Josie."

"But having the feeling is not something that we could tell you. You never would have believed us. You had to figure it out for yourself," said Jason.

Gabe stopped pacing the room and pulled a hand down his face. "I know you're right, I just wish I hadn't left. Look at all the time together we lost because I was so stupid."

Silence greeted the statement.

He looked between his brothers and saw nearly the same expression on their faces. Both had tilted their heads and cocked an eyebrow. "You could at least pretend to disagree with me."

"What for?" asked Jason. "You were an idiot but you couldn't see that.

A scream from Josie followed by curses upon his head sounded from the other room.

Gabe turned his head toward the bedroom where Josie was and cringed at the sound of her scream. "I hope she doesn't remember what she's saying. She'll never let me near her again."

Jason and Drew both laughed.

Drew clapped Gabe on the back. "She won't remember or care about anything but that baby once that child is in her arms."

"That's right," said Jason. "All will be forgotten and forgiven."

Suddenly the sounds from the room quieted. He heard neither Josie nor a baby. His gut clenched and he started for the bedroom afraid all of his fears came true. Then, through the quiet, a baby's cry issued forth.

Gabe ran to the bedroom and stopped in the doorway. She looked exhausted, her damp hair plastered to her face and yet, she was absolutely radiant. He walked to her, tucked a lock of hair behind her ear, then leaned down and kissed her ever so gently.

He wanted to mash his lips against hers and taste her with his tongue. He had such pride that she loved him and gave him a family. He wanted to mark her as his mate, but he realized he needed to be gentle with his wife. So, he kissed her tenderly before looking into her lap and seeing his baby. His son.

"Thank you," she said.

"For what?"

"For coming back. For finally realizing you loved me and for returning in time to make us legal and your son legitimate."

A sensation of relief traveled through him. Everything fell into place perfectly. "Why didn't anyone tell me?"

"I wouldn't let them. After you left, I got your family together and told them and swore them to secrecy. I didn't want you coming back just for the baby. I needed you to come back because you loved me." She smiled reached up and caressed his cheek. "And you did."

He sat next to her on the edge of the bed and looked down on his son. She held the baby lying naked in her lap. Together they counted his fingers and toes, ran their fingers through his downy blond hair.

"He's beautiful. Thank you."

"You're welcome."

The baby started to fuss. He kicked his legs and scrunched up his face. Then he opened his mouth, and a tiny cry issued forth.

Gabe chuckled. "I'm amazed I could hear that from the other room."

"We're really parents now. We'll hear his little cry as though he was a bull moose calling to his mate. Speaking of children, did you stop at the Eggleston's to see the kids?"

"No, I came directly here. I had to see you first." *The kids have probably grown so much I won't recognize them.*

"We need to let them know. They will want to be here to see their new brother. They still consider themselves our kids, which pleases me."

"I'll go in a bit. What will we name this little guy?"

"I thought about Brad. Bradley Dean Talbot. What do you think?"

"I think it's a perfect name for a perfect son."

Josie gazed up at the man she loved. Finally he realized he loved her. Now they were finally together in love. And it had been worth the wait.

Epilogue

Four years later

Mattie twirled in front of Josie's mirror in her wedding gown. The cheval mirror was a gift from Gabe and stood in their bedroom.

The dress Mattie wore was the same gown her Aunt Doris had worn and her mother had worn. Before that the gown had belonged to Mattie's great-grandmother.

Mattie had grown womanly curves in the last two years, though with the style of the dress, no one would be able to see. Except for her bosom which was on display in the design of the garment.

The dress had an empire waistline with a ribbon underneath her bust and then the skirt fell straight to the ground. Little puffed shoulders sat at the top of a long sleeve straight to just past her wrists. A little cleavage showed above the top of the neckline, but not too much. The color was a pale pink and looked wonderful with her dark red hair.

She asked her uncle to walk her down the aisle because Gabe was Lucas' best man, just as Josie was her matron of honor.

"You were pregnant at this time of year four years ago when Gabe came back from Massachusetts. Do you remember?" Mattie adjusted her sleeves a little so they didn't cover her ring. Lucas had given her a beautiful diamond engagement ring and she liked to show it off. She wore it on her right hand today so her wedding band would be the first on her finger.

"Of course, I remember. Apparently, early June is my time of year to be expecting. Do I embarrass you?"

Mattie took Josie's hand and squeezed it. "Never. It was just an observation. Looks like you have a new dress for the occasion."

She'd be worried if she knew my contractions had already started.

"Rachel sewed it for me. I've found the more she sews for me the better each garment fits. Of course, the fact that I now hold still for measurements probably has something to do with that. The hem is a difficult thing because I never know how big I'll get, or how much it will need to be let down in front so my ankles don't show."

"Well, the golden color is perfect with your sable hair and brown eyes. You almost outshine the bride."

"Angling for a compliment, are we? Well, you deserve one. You look absolutely gorgeous."

Mattie smiled. "Thanks. I did need some reassurance. I'm so nervous. Look at this." She held up her shaking hand. "It's a good thing Luke will be holding my left hand when he puts the ring on or he wouldn't be able to I'm trembling so badly."

"I know you're eighteen and fully grown now, but did Doris tell you about what happens on your wedding night?"

Mattie blushed from her forehead to her toes. "Yes, she did. I'm fully prepared…well, at least I'm not scared. I know Luke loves me and I love him, so everything will be all right."

"Good." Josie lifted her head. *Mattie has come so far from the dirty girl Gabe and I found in that cabin. She's so smart. I'm so proud of her.* "I hear the music so I'll go out now. You count to five and follow me."

Josie got to the podium in front of the reverend and turned to watch Mattie. She walked down the aisle, holding her uncle George's arm and she glowed. Her smile was wide and she kept her eyes on Luke.

Josie turned and gazed at her husband. Gabe wore a three piece suit with cravat. His vest was silver brocade and looked marvelous with the black suit. He'd slicked back his hair but, as the hair dried, curls formed around his neckline. Curls she loved to run her fingers through.

As the reverend finished the ceremony, and Luke and Mattie kissed, Josie was hard-pressed not to kiss her husband, as well. When they joined everyone outside, after the ceremony, she couldn't hold back any longer.

"Do you know how handsome you look today?"

"No, but you are absolutely beautiful."

"Mama!"

Brad and his little sister, Colleen, ran toward her from Rachel's side.

She'd been surprised that they'd stayed with their aunt through the wedding.

"Hi, my sweethearts. How are you?"

"I'm a good boy." Brad was the image of his father with dark blond hair and blue eyes. At four years old, he was already tall and looked like he was six.

"I good, too." Colleen had her daddy's blue eyes but her mother's brown hair. She was a chubby little thing and her daddy's little angel.

"Yes, you have been very good children."

"Can we have a candy stick? Aunt Lucy has some but said we have to ask first."

"You two have been so good today that you most certainly can have one. But just one. Okay?"

"Okay."

"'K" said Colleen, following her brother as fast as her chubby little legs would carry her.

They ran back to their aunt.

Gabe stood behind and wrapped his arms around her resting them on atop tummy.

Shaking her head Josie sighed. "He's growing up so fast. I close my eyes and he's an inch taller. Soon, he'll tower over me, just like his father. And Colleen, she's almost as bad as he is. Look how she runs"

"Perhaps, but we'll have a new baby shortly and you'll be glad they're as grown up as they are."

She leaned back against him. The contractions had started during a particularly bad night. She'd had a nightmare that Gabe had left her and was gone. Josie knew the dream was simply her insecurity working its way to the surface. Even after all these years, she still had inklings of fear that he would leave.

A hard contraction hit.

Gabe moved his hands over her stomach. "How long have you been in labor?"

"Since about midnight."

He turned her in his arms. "Don't you think we should go home and get ready to meet our new child?"

"I suppose. I didn't want to miss Mattie's wedding."

"You haven't but now is the time to leave. Can you walk to the buggy?"

"I think so. Let's just let this pain pass and then we can go."

Gabe kissed the top of her head and then bent and kissed her neck. She knew she should scold him for being so forward in public, but she didn't. Today was Mattie's wedding, and she wouldn't call any more attention to them.

"We can go now."

Gabe released her and then held his arm out for her.

She placed her hand through the crook of his elbow and held up two fingers so Rachel knew the baby was coming, then they walked slowly to the buggy. It seemed that everything she did lately was slowly. She felt as big as the side of a barn. This child was going to be a big baby. She was carrying it so much heavier than the other two.

Just as they got to the buggy, she stopped and grabbed onto the seat. Josie cringed as liquid dampened her undergarments.

"My water just broke. I guess we are leaving none too soon."

Gabe scooped her into his arms and lifted her into the buggy.

"I'll get you situated at home and then go for Karen."

"We don't need Karen yet. I'll let you know when." She tried to settle on the seat, but wished she wasn't sitting in wet clothes.

He raised an eyebrow. "I'd be more comfortable if she was there, but you know best."

The longer the ride home took the more uncomfortable she got. The pain was like the contraction never quit.

"You had better get Karen after all. Something's different about this baby. I feel like he's coming right now."

Gabe whipped the horses into a gallop and reached the house in no time. They had built a new house on the mountain near Jason's and Drew's. Josie loved her home. Gabe had consulted her in the design process, so it had just five bedrooms, a large pantry and kitchen with space for eating.

Gabe pulled the horses to a stop in front of the house, closer to the stairs to the bedroom.

When they gave Rachel the sign at the wedding, she was to tell Lucy, so she and Drew would take Brad and Colleen home with them. They didn't have to worry about them right now.

"Everything will be all right. I'll get Karen just as soon as I see you're settled." Gabe carried her up the porch steps into the house and on up the stairs to the bedroom.

"Are you all right for me to get Karen?"

"Yes, I'll be fine, but don't dawdle."

He kissed her. "Wouldn't think of it."

Two days ago, Josie had prepared the bed and they'd been sleeping on a sheet over the oil cloth since. Now, she stripped the bed of the blankets and left only the sheets.

After the next contraction, she undid the buttons of her skirt—a new design with the sides of the skirt brought up and crossed over her stomach and buttoned under her bosom. This way, the dress could be worn for a long time through her pregnancy just by adjusting the placement of the buttons. The bodice buttoned down the front so the dress could be worn after pregnancy and used to nurse.

She laid the dress over the top of the privacy screen. The dress was followed by her chemise and bloomers. Then she donned her nightgown. She'd bought this one four sizes too large to accommodate her expanding belly and it still fit snug over her stomach.

Before she climbed into the four-poster bed that she'd talked Gabe into, she fluffed the pillows behind where she would lay and grabbed the novel she was reading, *The Scarlet Letter* by Nathanial Hawthorne. She would read a bit until Gabe got back. Then they could discuss the child's names. They had decided on George and Doris, but Josie had since decided she didn't like those names, even if they were the names of Mattie's aunt and uncle, who had become dear friends.

No she wanted something different. She liked Edward for a boy. Edward Gabriel Talbot.

And for a girl she wanted Helen.

Another contraction hit, and she could swear she felt the baby's head starting to come out.

Fifteen minutes later Gabe and Karen arrived.

Karen walked in with her big medical bag and set it on the bureau where she had room to open it. "Well, that baby decided to show up, did he?"

"Yes, sooner than anticipated. Karen, I think the baby is already coming. I can feel his head."

Karen went to the commode and washed her hands in the basin there.

"Okay, that could be happening. Sometimes second and third children come quickly. Lie back and raise your knees."

Josie wanted very much to push and was having a difficult time not doing so. With a moan at the movement, she raised her knees and opened them wide.

"Well, I'll be," said Karen. "You were right this baby is coming. I want you to push now. Hard. Push. Push. Push." She put her hand on Josie's leg. "Rest now. Gabe, see if Rachel or Margaret are here yet and put some water on to heat so we can clean the baby."

Gabe went to Josie, kissed her lips and squeezed her hand. "You're doing great sweetheart."

"Gabe. The water."

"Yes, ma'am."

He left.

Karen said, "Okay push again, that's it. He's coming quickly. Push. Rest. Rest. Now give me one final push. Hard. Press down hard."

Josie grabbed the bed post and pushed as hard as she could. In short order she felt the baby slip from her body.

"You have a boy," said Karen. She caught the baby in a towel, wiped out his mouth with her finger, held him by his feet and swatted him on the butt. The baby let out a cry.

"I'm here now, I'll take him," said Rachel as she rushed into the room.

"Karen, something is wrong. I need to push again. I think I'm having another baby."

Karen pushed her legs wide again.

"Well, I'll be damned. Excuse my language, but you are having another one and he's already coming. Push now, Josie. Push hard."

She did, pushed with all her might, and in short order, the second baby was born. A girl this time.

"What do you want to name her?" asked Karen.

"Helen," said Josie. "Helen Rene Talbot.

Rachel handed little Edward, all cleaned up, to his mother and then took Helen from Karen.

Karen smiled. "You are amazing. You carried those babies full term. That's unusual for twins. Usually bed rest is required."

Josie heard heavy boots coming up the stairs.

Gabe came in carrying two buckets. "I brought one of hot water and a bucket of cold, too"

"Sweetheart," said Josie. "Come and meet your new son, Edward Gabriel Talbot."

"That's not the name we chose, but I like it. I didn't particularly care for George and Doris either."

After both babies were cleaned up, Karen and Rachel left.

"Isn't her little mouth the cutest." Josie held Helen who was loosely covered with a blanket after her parent's inspection. "We'll have our hands full, you know that don't you?"

"Twins?" Gabe took a step back.

"Twins!" repeated Josie.

He leaned down, kissed Josie and then kissed Helen whose hair was as blonde and downy as her brother's was. "You know, but I wouldn't have it any other way. Would you?"

"No. Our children are proof of our love." Warmth invaded her chest and her heart was so full of love for her family and her husband. "I do love you so very much. Kiss me again."

"With pleasure, my love. With pleasure."

ABOUT THE AUTHOR

CYNTHIA WOOLF is the award winning and best-selling author of twenty-five historical western romance books and two short stories with more books on the way.

Cynthia loves writing and reading romance. Her first western romance, *Tame A Wild Heart*, was inspired by the story her mother told her of meeting Cynthia's father on a ranch in Creede, Colorado. Although *Tame A Wild Heart* takes place in Creede that is the only similarity between the stories. Her father was a cowboy not a bounty hunter and her mother was a nursemaid (called a nanny now) not the ranch owner. The ranch they met on is still there as part of the open space in Mineral County in southwestern Colorado.

Writing as CA Woolf, she has six sci-fi, space opera romance titles. She calls them westerns in space.

Cynthia credits her wonderfully supportive husband Jim and her critique partners for saving her sanity and allowing her to explore her creativity.

WEBSITE – http://cynthiawoolf.com
NEWSLETTER – http://bit.ly/1qBWhFQ

Made in the USA
Middletown, DE
05 July 2021

43646683R00136